AF584745

Kiss and Repeat

Kiss and Repeat

HEATHER TRUETT

Swoon READS
New York

A Swoon Reads Book
An imprint of Feiwel and Friends and Macmillan Publishing Group, LLC
120 Broadway, New York, NY 10271

Our books may be purchased in bulk for promotional, educational, or business use. Please contact your local bookseller or the Macmillan Corporate and Premium Sales Department at (800) 221-7945 ext. 5442 or by email at MacmillanSpecialMarkets@macmillan.com.

Library of Congress Cataloging-in-Publication Data is available.

ISBN 978-1-250-26292-9 (hardcover)

Book design by Mike Burroughs

First edition, 2021

10 9 8 7 6 5 4 3 2 1

fiercereads.com

For Chris, wherever you are riding now

This is the kind of life I've had.
Drunk, and in charge of a bicycle,
as an Irish police report once put it.
Drunk with life, that is, and not knowing where off to next.
But you're on your way before dawn. And the trip?
Exactly one half terror, exactly one half exhilaration.

—Ray Bradbury, *Zen in the Art of Writing*

Chapter One

It was tradition for a junior to host the end of summer bash, and Ballard was the obvious pick. He had everything a good party host needed: a giant lake house, easy access to alcohol, and parents who worked more than they breathed.

I borrowed Mom's car to make the thirty-minute trek to Lake Martin, freshly shaved and worried I went a bit too heavy-handed with the cologne. I kept the windows down to air myself out and tried not to stress about the night ahead.

Beside me on the seat, my phone buzzed, but I ignored it until I parked.

Where are you? It was Ballard.

I rolled up the windows and turned up the air-conditioning while I took three deep breaths. Then I replied, *Outside. In the car.*

Well get out of the car. You said you wanted to have more fun this year. It's a party. Have fun.

For Ballard, it was that simple. Show up. Have fun.

I'm coming in. Probably. Just give me a second.

Ok. I'm putting my phone away now. This is your call.

To party or not to party? Should that even be a question? I took one more deep breath, turned off the engine, and got out of the car.

Of course, I ran into Wade Bond not three feet from the front door. His blond hair was spiked in front like some boy band heartthrob, a girl in an American flag T-shirt draped across his arm.

"Hey there, Luckie." Wade's foot shot in front of me. I wasn't quick enough to dodge it, but I managed a little jump and turn, so I didn't fall flat on my face. Years of practice improved my balance when it came to recovering from bully-foot-in-the-path.

The girl with him laughed, and Wade called after me, "Where you off to so fast? You need to see the wizard?"

I flipped him the bird, but only because it was dark and he couldn't see me anymore. I would stand up to Wade eventually, but not while he was drunk. That wouldn't be smart.

In the living room, I spotted Erin Mielke and her latest boyfriend. She waved, and I stopped to say hi.

Erin and I met in first grade. I hid under her desk during a meltdown and she screamed and told the teacher I was looking up her dress.

That was in Auburn, where my mom used to be an associate pastor and Erin's mom was finishing a master's degree. Erin's family went to our church and, when Mom was reappointed to Moorhen to start The Exchange, she hired Brian, Erin's dad, as her worship pastor. His wife got a job teaching art, thanks to amazing timing—what Mom would call God's timing.

And there we were, Erin and me, growing up in the same churches, playing tag around the same pews, setting up endless games of Monopoly while our parents planned every aspect of The Exchange for years and years.

"This is Miles," Erin said, gesturing to the guy beside her.

Miles and I nodded at one another. We'd seen each other around school, but I didn't know much about him.

I joined Miles and some other guys playing *Call of Duty* on the big screen and zoned out for a bit.

By ten o'clock, the music was loud and the people around me were louder. Since I was sober, I remember more of that night than anyone else. Ballard's reddish-orange hair flared on the back deck and I followed the signal. Mostly I'd stayed with the *Call of Duty* group, but nervous energy made me restless.

I hadn't run into Wade since I first arrived, but that couldn't last. This was a party, and Wade was one of the gods of the Moorhen High football team. He wouldn't stay on the fringes for long.

"Yo, Stephen!" Ballard hollered from his Adirondack throne, a Solo cup held out like an offering. Wade may have been a football god, but Ballard was still king of this party.

I stepped into the golden glow of a lantern that hung above our heads, hands in my pockets to keep my newest tic from drawing attention. My fingers flexed involuntarily and I gritted my teeth.

"Here." Ballard pushed the cup toward me and I waved it away.

He knew I wouldn't drink it, not while on the kind of meds I take. Still, he pushed it at me again, and I shook my head in refusal. He was like that when people were around, less my friend and more the cool class clown.

"He doesn't want it," someone said.

I glanced around the group. It was Joan Pearson. I'd

looked right past her earlier, not recognizing her with newly dyed black hair. Her hair used to be a soft brown. She had these piercing dark eyes, and she narrowed them in Ballard's direction, defending me. She had a bit of a messiah complex going on.

"I can speak for myself," I said.

A sudden thump of bass from the speakers drowned me out, NF's quick tongue shooting lyrics like arrows all over the deck. Joan tossed back raven hair and sipped from her own Solo cup. Ballard shrugged and turned his attention back to the others.

Erin and Miles stepped out of the house and made their way to where I was standing. Some friends were there, plus a couple of girls I didn't recognize, and Joan's friend Sylvie. Sylvie was showing this guy, Andrew, something on her phone.

"Awesome," Andrew said, grinning. "Let's play."

"Play what?" one of the girls asked. Her hair was curly and damp, like she'd just been for a swim.

"Sylvie found this app like spin the bottle." Andrew waved the phone in our direction, its glittery red case catching the lantern light.

"We put everyone's name and picture into the app," Sylvie explained. "Then we spin the virtual bottle and it tells us who to kiss."

"That's boring," this guy, Case, said. "If I wanted to kiss any girl here, I'd do it. I don't need an app for that." Case didn't need alcohol to act like an idiot, but he'd had some.

"I dare you," Ballard said. He motioned with his cup as

a group of girls walked up the steps. One of them wore a Tallassee High T-shirt and I figured that's why I didn't recognize half the people there. They were from nearby towns, crashing from some other party at someone else's lake house.

Lake Martin was surrounded by tiny Alabama towns full of tiny Alabama lives. One day, I'd get the hell out of this place for sure.

"Pick a girl," Case demanded, unable to turn down a dare. "Any girl."

"Her." Ballard pointed at one of the new arrivals. She wore jean shorts and a yellow bikini top. I stared a little too long. My foot jerked twice, fast, and I fell into the chair next to Ballard. No one noticed, too intent on Case and the girl.

Case tried to march across the deck, but he'd had a few too many and swayed as he went. The girl turned when he planted himself beside her. Case leaned forward, but the look on the girl's face was enough to make him back down.

We laughed so hard I pulled my hands out of my pockets to hold my sides. Ballard spilled his beer on my shoes, and Joan said something to Sylvie, something that sounded like "assholes."

Case didn't bother coming back to the group. He went into the house, hunting for another beer to drown his humiliation. I wasn't sorry for him. He had to know he deserved it. I'd never kissed anyone, but even if I'd kissed a million girls, I couldn't imagine walking up to one and laying it on her.

Maybe I was naive.

Okay, I know I was naive, but I was positive I could never be as big of a jerk as Case Malone.

"Hey, great party, man." Another guy joined our circle, reaching over to fist-bump Ballard.

We were an odd combination, Ballard's court of fools. Andrew was a junior like me, an okay guy. Joan was a tough girl, smart and always angry for no known reason. She had this existential angst factor that kept her from fitting in much of anywhere, but she used to date Wade. He was her ticket into any group—him and Sylvie. Sylvie was one of those all-around friendly people. She could fit in comfortably anywhere. Beautiful, with white-blond hair and round honey-brown eyes, like some kind of angel, Sylvie was welcome wherever she went. None of us had dated her, but we all daydreamed about it, unable to ignore the shape of her in tight jeans and a red sweater. Red was her color. She always wore something red.

"Come on, let's play." Sylvie called our attention back to her, and we all willingly gave it. If Ballard was king that night, Sylvie was queen.

"All right, set it up," Ballard told her, leaning forward in his chair.

"We're out," Erin said, giving me a little wave as she wandered away with Miles.

"What're we playing?" A new guy, Michael, dropped into a seat. I didn't know him well, but I recognized him from the football team. His presence made me nervous, because usually the football boys hung together. So if this guy was here, Wade would appear soon. The idea of dealing with Wade made my fingers flex like crazy. I stuck my hands back in my pockets.

Sylvie explained the game and the guys complained it was boring. "Just a kiss? Some stupid little peck on the cheek?"

It didn't sound boring to me, but those guys had rounded home while I was still in the dugout. I glanced around and caught a girl from school watching me. Her nose was crinkled up, like she'd smelled something bad. I blushed, thinking she was worried about playing this game with me, about having to maybe kiss me.

A few more girls joined the group, bringing another football player with them. Someone called someone else a prude. Joan rolled her eyes, and I forgot about the spin-the-bottle app. I watched Joan.

I was always watching Joan, and the black hair made me see her in all kinds of new ways. Her skin glistened underneath the lantern light. Her tank top revealed the edge of her lime-green bra, its elastic strap falling off one shoulder.

I'd loved Joan for four years.

I'd also hated Joan for four years.

When I looked up from the neckline of Joan's tank top, her eyes were on me, and my cheeks burned. I expected anger, her usual, but instead she sighed, shook her head, and whispered something in Sylvie's ear.

"So we change the rules," Michael said. "We up the stakes." He was a quarterback, used to calling the plays.

"What is this? Poker?" Joan asked. I forced myself to focus and not get caught staring again.

"Better. Instead of a kiss, you go in a bedroom with whoever's name pops up." Michael wiggled his eyebrows. It was supposed to be suggestive, but he looked silly. His nose was a bit big for his face, and he had a zit right under his left eye. But it didn't matter, because he was an athlete. If you could throw a damn ball halfway down a field, you were golden.

I couldn't throw a ball halfway down a hill.

"Ew, no." Sylvie wrinkled her nose. "I'm not having sex with someone because an app tells me to."

This made Ballard laugh again, his face bright red and then purple. I slapped him on the back.

"Not sex," Michael said in a tone that would've made me feel like an idiot but of which Sylvie was unaware. "Just go in the bedroom for five minutes. We'll never know what you do in there."

My hands were sweating. My fingers flexed once, twice, three times. I shoved them deeper in my pockets. I had to get out of there before the game started. Getting off the sidelines had been a terrible idea.

"I'm in," the curly-haired girl said.

Everyone else started talking at once, and Sylvie shushed them. "I need to take everyone's picture and put it with their name."

I stood up, planning to return to *Call of Duty*, a game I could handle, but it was too late.

"Look, Stephen volunteers to go first," Ballard said.

A breeze lifted his empty cup and scuttled it across the deck. I watched it go and was jealous. Jealous of a damn cup, because it got to leave and I didn't.

"All righty, Stephen, smile." Sylvie snapped my photo.

Just like that, I was playing a kissing game with a group that included Joan Pearson.

I sat back down. My foot jerked, my fingers flexed, and my mouth did the grimace. I hate the grimace. It's a twisting of my lips so fast and harsh it leaves them sore. I wanted to cover my mouth with one hand, but my flexing fingers made it impossible.

That's how my body reacts to stress. I have Tourette's syndrome, and my medication makes the tics manageable, but as soon as I get a bit anxious, my muscles rally into action.

I turned my face away from the light and tried not to cry while Sylvie went around the circle, snapping pictures and typing names. Her tongue poked from the corner of her mouth in concentration.

The crying is another thing. It used to be bad. I'd cry over anything, and there's nothing NOT humiliating about being a boy known for sobbing in class. I took a few deep breaths and suffered through another grimace before the game started.

I rarely got to be this close to Joan, and the last thing I wanted her to notice me for was my tics. At that moment, I would have given anything to make them stop. Forever or just for the night.

Joan kept looking around. Probably for Wade.

Wade, douchiest of douchelords.

Michael volunteered to spin first, and the virtual bottle landed on one of the girls I didn't know. She followed Michael into the house, short skirt swinging against tan thighs.

Around me, people laughed and talked, trying to be heard over the music. NF had given way to something slower by Drake. Solo cups littered the deck and wind rustled tree limbs. Ballard's mom had at least ten sets of wind chimes hanging in the trees, maybe more. Some were metal, and some were crystal, and all of them were singing.

When Michael and the girl hadn't come back after five minutes, Sylvie decided to take her turn, tapping the phone screen and glancing around at each of our faces. The app whirred, and just when it seemed there was a glitch, it dinged.

"Stephen," Sylvie chirped, her voice on pitch with the nearest set of chimes. They were copper, swinging into view behind her head.

Ballard shoved me and said something I didn't understand. My heart thumped louder than the bass line. Sylvie was already crossing the deck, and my fingers flexed so many times I lost count. I made fists in my jean pockets as I followed her into the house and up a flight of carpeted stairs. Behind me, the guys were hooting and calling encouragement.

The only empty room belonged to Ballard's little sister. The bedspread was aqua with bright flowers. Barbies littered the floor.

"Ouch." Sylvie was barefoot and stopped to rub her heel. A pink plastic shoe was the culprit. My foot jerked. If she noticed, she didn't show it.

"I've never kissed a girl."

I blurted that out. Go me. Smooth operator.

Sylvie smiled, her lips shiny with gloss. She sat on the edge of the bed and patted the place beside her. I sat and listened to my own heart.

The music was quiet up here. Sylvie was wearing a red sundress, her hair long enough to fountain over her shoulders and frame the first set of breasts I'd ever been close enough to touch.

I imagined touching them. I bet they'd be soft and light, like Sylvie.

My foot jerked.

My fingers flexed.

And she kissed me.

I didn't have time to make an awkward first move. Her lips were sticky from the gloss, and she tasted like raspberries and mint gum. She put her hands on my wrists and pulled them out of my pockets. Potential finger flexes forgotten, I wrapped one arm around her waist and pulled her closer. I touched her white-gold hair and it was like feathers.

She pushed her tongue against my lips. Her fingers curled into my hair and I pressed against her, tilting her back. My body was ahead of me, brain picturing her lying on the bed, how it would feel to peel her shirt off.

That didn't happen.

Instead, she resisted my push and our lips parted. She looked me in the eye and gave her same sweet smile from earlier.

"I hope your first kiss was pleasant," she said.

It's the kind of dreamy-voiced thing Sylvie was known for saying. She spoke a bit like somebody's grandma, but with her face and body, none of us cared how she talked. She could speak Swedish, and we'd hang on her every un-understandable word.

Back on the deck, Ballard waggled his eyebrows and asked me how it was. I blushed and didn't answer. I was strangely calm, and I wanted to hold on to that feeling.

"It was lovely," Sylvie told our crew, another thing none of the other girls would ever say after a make-out session. She looked at me with those light brown eyes, all soft and happy. "I'm tempted to rig the game so I get to kiss him again."

I met her gaze as Ballard passed me the phone. She winked.

Fingers shaking, I tapped the screen and let it whir. Once again, it seemed to take forever.

And then, as though God was smiling on me, blessing this preacher's kid with a night of dreams come true, the app dinged. There was a name and a picture.

"Who is it?" Ballard asked. "Did it land back on Sylvie, you lucky asswad?"

I looked across the circle, nervous and conflicted.

"Joan," I said.

She wasn't paying attention, her neck craned to see over my head.

Sylvie reached to tap Joan's shoulder, but it was too late. The Thor of Moorhen High had made his way to the back deck.

"Wade," Joan called. "We're over here."

"I'm leaving," he shouted over the music. "Wanna come?"

"Sure," she answered.

Joan tugged at Sylvie and Sylvie slid her feet into the sandals by her chair. She took her phone from my fingers and followed Joan to where Wade stood. The three of them disappeared.

The game was over.

In the silence between songs, I heard the chimes again. They sounded like bitter disappointment . . . and relief.

The evening went on and people moved all around me, but I stayed in my seat on the deck, watching those copper chimes. Something was niggling at the back of my brain, something important I couldn't put my finger on.

Later, when I was driving Mom's car home with five drunk people stuffed in the backseat (my meds made me the designated driver by default), my fingers flexed on the steering wheel. Flex, flex, flex.

And it hit me.

I walked into that bedroom twitching. But as soon as Sylvie's lips touched mine, I was still. Not one tic while we were kissing.

Not. One. Tic.

Chapter Two

Sunday afternoon, Ballard showed up at my house after church. His family went to the early service at First Baptist. He'd already changed from church clothes into navy athletic shorts and an Auburn T-shirt. I motioned him inside and changed while he filled me in on the post-party gossip.

Girls are the ones with a reputation for talking about people, but Ballard could give them a run for their money. He knew things about people I'd have never figured out. Some of it he learned from his parents, who learned it from their friends, who were the parents of our classmates.

Moorhen is not a big town, and Ballard's dad was born and raised here. He's related to so many people, Ballard always has to ask if some girl is his cousin before he sets his sights on her. It sounds like a joke, but he asked a girl out once and discovered they were related. I'm the only one who knows about it.

"What about Joan and Wade?" I asked, keeping my tone casual. "Are they back together now?"

"What? Why?" Ballard thought I hated Joan. He was clueless about the part of me that found her fascinating, the part of me that desperately wanted to be cool enough to steal her attention away from Wade.

"Well, they left together, didn't they?" I tossed my collared shirt in the direction of the hamper and missed.

Ballard shrugged. "They probably hooked up or something. Wade's dating a girl from Montgomery. I met her last week, at the mall."

I dropped into my desk chair and made no comment on Wade's girlfriend activity. If I'd said anything, Ballard would've ragged me for it. He was always pointing out my prudishness and blaming it on my mom. She's a minister, which is why we live in Moorhen. The United Methodist Conference sent her to start a church here when I was in seventh grade.

Also, it's a well-known fact I hate everything about Wade Bond, from his stupidly deep voice to his dirty-blond hair. We're talking about a guy who introduces himself by saying, "My name's Bond, Wade Bond."

How original.

Wade started mocking my tics the moment I appeared at Moorhen Middle School. He'd flap his arms like a chicken and cluck when I walked by. I used to do this little hop when I moved fast. My legs would jerk and it made me sort of jump in the air, like I was skipping happily across a meadow or some shit. Wade would link his arm in mine and drag me down the hall singing, "We're off to see the wizard, the fucking wizard of Oz." Real creative, that guy.

"What about you and Sylvie?" Ballard lay on my bed, absentmindedly spinning the propeller on a model airplane I hadn't touched in years. It still needed its right wing.

"What about me and Sylvie?" My face went hot at the memory of raspberry lip gloss and mint gum, but I was a little bit pleased he asked. Ballard was the one who told stories about girls. I was the one who listened. It's how our friendship had always worked.

"Oh come off it, you know what about you and Sylvie. Sylvie never kisses high school boys, at least not any we know. And when she suddenly decided to try it, you landed in a bedroom with her. Door locked."

"We didn't lock the door," I said, fingers flexing on the arms of my chair.

He threw a pillow at me, and I ducked so it hit the wall and landed on my desk, pencils and game controllers scattering noisily.

"How far'd y'all go, man? I'm dying over here." Ballard grabbed his chest like his heart might give out.

My mouth twisted. Ballard didn't point it out.

"I didn't have any tics," I told him, my realization from the night before bouncing from brain to lips. "When I was kissing Sylvie, they all stopped."

"Seriously? Is that normal?" Ballard sat up on the bed.

"How would I know? I never kissed anyone before last night."

"You're sure, though? Maybe you're so used to them, you didn't notice."

"Uh-uh," I said. "My fingers didn't flex in her hair or anything. They were bad last night, because I was nervous."

"I know. Your foot was jerking before y'all went upstairs." If he still noticed my tics after all these years, everyone else must've noticed them too. If I could just hold still, I could fit in with the other guys, be the kind of guy that might win Joan Pearson.

"Yeah," I agreed. "I was afraid my mouth would do something weird when we were kissing, ya know? Like she'd feel my lips go all funny."

"But they didn't?" Ballard asked.

"They didn't. We kissed, and I didn't even think about Tourette's. I don't know how long we were in there, but it was the best however many minutes of my life."

Ballard gave a serious nod, and in this conversation, it was clear why we stayed friends even after our shared interests veered in wildly different directions. Ballard was a good listener when he wanted to be, and he knew me better than anyone.

We were both quiet for a while, Ballard spinning the propeller and me thinking about Sylvie. Or not about Sylvie, only about how it was to be with her, my muscles not commandeering my focus.

Ballard broke the silence with, "Did she let you touch her boobs?"

I picked up the pillow from my desk and lobbed it across the room. It hit him in the head. "He shoots. He scores."

Laughing, Ballard popped the pillow behind him and leaned against the headboard. "Maybe it's a treatment?"

"A treatment?"

"Yeah, a therapy method," he said. "I mean maybe kissing could stop your tics, like your meds, but better."

I shook my head. "Nah, the tics came back in the car driving home. Not bad, just how they are when I drive, subdued but present. And it might've been a fluke. I mean, I've never kissed anyone else. Maybe the next time I kiss a girl, my whole body will jerk and she'll run screaming from the room."

I was making a joke, but I also sort of meant it. The idea of having sex one day made me sweat and shake all over. I could develop tics involving just about every muscle in my body, so why not that super important muscle I'd need in full working order . . . My bat would need to stay steady if I ever expected to hit a homerun. I found no unembarrassing way to explain my fear, so I kept it to myself.

Ballard paused his propeller spinning and cocked his head to one side.

I knew that look. My best friend had an idea. It might be a good idea, but it would still land us in trouble. And it would probably be worth it.

"What we have here is a hypothesis," Ballard said.

"Man, quit it. We've got one more day before school starts. I don't want to do science."

He held up a hand to silence my protests. "We have a hypothesis that says kissing makes your tics stop. Right?"

I sighed, resigned. "Right, a hypothesis."

"That's step one of the scientific method." Ballard grabbed a notebook from my bedside table. "Got a pen?"

I tossed him a pen. "That's not step one. You skipped two steps."

"Okay, smart-ass, what's step one?"

"Step one is purpose," I said. "And step two is research."

"Fine. The purpose is to treat Tourette's. Or pause it. Or whatever the hell you want. Calm your body. That's our purpose."

He had me. I was listening.

"Research is done. Making out with Sylvie was research,

and if that was the kind of lab assignment they handed out in class, I would be the geekiest damn nerd in Moorhen."

I couldn't help but agree. If any of my classes involved following consenting girls into empty bedrooms, I'd be way more willing to hit the books.

"Step three. Our hypothesis is kissing pauses your tics." Ballard made notes in his neat block handwriting. "I barely passed science, so go ahead and tell me if I'm wrong, but isn't step four experiment?"

"Bingo." My nerves vibrated under my skin. I could read the smirk forming on Ballard's face.

"So, here's the plan. You are going to kiss another girl. And, because one girl doesn't give us a whole lot of data to analyze, you're going to kiss another. And another. And another. You're going to kiss any girl you can until we have an answer."

"There's a problem here," I interjected.

"What?" Ballard looked up from his paper.

"In sixteen years of life, I've gotten exactly one girl to kiss me, and that's only thanks to a stupid phone app."

"Good point." Ballard chewed my pen. Gross.

"Unless you can convince everyone to play kissing games all the time, I'm screwed."

"How about you leave the girl acquisition to me? I'll land you some chicks. You kiss them." Ballard spun the pen around his fingers.

"And how will you come up with all these girls?" I raised an eyebrow.

"I don't know," he said. "But I'm Ballard Keighley. I can

always get girls to like me, so I just gotta figure out how to do the same for you."

Mom poked her head in the room a few minutes later. "Hey, Ballard, wanna stay for lunch?"

She'd changed out of the yellow dress she'd worn to church and into an old T-shirt and jeans. The tiny cross tattoo on her wrist peeked out beneath her watch.

"Sure, Mrs. Luckie," Ballard said. "Thanks for inviting me."

We spent the rest of the afternoon playing *Minecraft*, a game Ballard would never admit to liking anywhere outside of my house. Ballard didn't have to be cool around me. He could just be Ballard.

Once Ballard headed home, I was left to think about his plan for a kissing experiment. It was intriguing, but also not likely to work. If my best friend went around asking girls to kiss me, that would be humiliating on so many levels.

I was sure stopping my tics was the key to my (lack of) girl problems, but I was also sure Ballard's experiment wasn't likely to end well for me.

Chapter Three

The first day of school was underwhelming. Ballard and I were excited to be upperclassmen, but nothing about Moorhen High was different from when we were underclassmen, as far as I could tell.

Except for Sylvie. Not Sylvie herself. I spotted her hanging around outside the auditorium before first period. She wore a red T-shirt, knotted at the waist, and one of those long skirts the girls were all into. It had a tribal print and hugged her hips real nice. Ballard caught me looking.

"There are rumors," he said.

I tore my eyes from Sylvie's tiny waist. "Rumors about what?"

"People saw you go into a bedroom with Sylvie." He grinned.

"It was a game," I reminded him. "No one will ever believe Sylvie likes me."

Ballard shrugged. "They're saying you got lucky. Pun intended."

Of course the pun was intended. Kids had always loved to twist my last name into all sorts of phrases. That first day of junior year, "Luckie got lucky" was the funniest thing they'd ever heard. Guys who normally ignored me altogether nodded in acknowledgment when I passed them in the hall.

"Nothing happened," I said again and again. I said it to Ballard, to Case, to Michael, and to every guy who smirked and offered me a high five as they passed my locker.

In the couple of minutes I spent kissing Sylvie, I went from lame loser to validated member of the man club, but I wasn't comfortable with it. My newfound status was built on Sylvie's battered reputation, which my gut told me wasn't okay. It made me angry, and I didn't handle anger well. It felt overwhelming and I spent a lot of that day taking deep breaths and fighting to keep my frustration in check.

"It's no big deal," Sylvie said when I broached the subject in math class, the Thursday after the party. "The people who matter know it's not true. And the people who don't matter . . . well . . . they don't matter." She was doodling a flower on the edge of her worksheet, but she paused to offer me an encouraging smile.

"I just don't like people thinking I'd use a girl, or that you would—"

"I get it, Stephen, I do. You're a good guy, but you can't control what other people think. Do you think I'm a slut?"

My cheeks burned. "No, of course not."

"Okay, then. You matter. They"—she gestured around the classroom—"don't."

"But I want to fix it, Sylvie. They shouldn't get to assume things about you or judge you."

"You're right. They shouldn't. But I don't need you to fix things for me. I'm not a damsel in distress. You are already telling them nothing happened. Keep doing that. I will keep doing that too."

Thanks to that conversation, I was more myself by lunchtime. It wasn't okay, no, but Sylvie was right. We were both honest about what did and didn't happen in that bedroom, and she didn't need me to protect her.

We sat down at a table in the cafeteria, where Joan and Sylvie were hunched over their phones, comparing Instagram photos, and Case was helping Andrew with Algebra II homework.

"Wanna bike Lost Bridge today?" I asked Ballard before biting into my sandwich.

I have to study," he said. "Chem quiz tomorrow. But we need to talk soon. I've been working on a plan for our kissing experiment."

As if on cue, Case glanced up, caught my eye, and said, "Luckie got lucky" with a grin.

I flipped him the bird and turned back to Ballard. "No, I'm not going to kiss a bunch of random girls. I've heard 'Luckie got lucky' enough to last a lifetime."

"No one has to know. Trust me."

I wanted to trust him. I first met Ballard in the guidance office. He was in trouble for goofing off, nothing unusual, and I was visiting a counselor about something in my 504 plan. A 504 plan is the pile of papers outlining different ways I get help because of Tourette's syndrome, like being allowed to take my exams in the library, away from other kids. My processing speed and style is different than a typical student's, and I have a lot of trouble blocking out sensory stimuli. I know it looks like "special treatment" to a lot of people, but those people have never lived inside my head.

Anyway, Ballard asked me straight up, "Why do you keep flinging your arms out?"

I told Ballard I had Tourette's. He said, "That sucks." I appreciated the assessment. No pity and no making fun of me. A week later, we ran into each other in the old mall parking lot, both of us using the decrepit sidewalks as bike paths.

We've been friends ever since.

So, I wanted to trust him, but I'd learned not to trust anyone with a "great idea" sure to get me in trouble. I always get caught doing the stupidest things. It's never worth it.

Example: The worship pastor's daughter, Erin Mielke, once convinced me it would be fun to light all the candles at church and play séance while our parents were in a meeting. The old lady who found us about had a heart attack.

"You never want to ride anymore," I complained, crumpling up a soda can and ignoring his appeal for trust.

"We're getting too old for bike riding." He shoved a fry into his mouth and I sighed. I didn't feel any older than I did sophomore year, and we rode our bikes plenty then, but at least we were off the subject of kissing experiments.

"Hey, Stephen," Joan called down the table.

"Yeah?" I turned in her direction.

"Did you write down the page numbers for English?"

"Sure. You need them?"

She nodded and I pulled a binder from my backpack, flipping until I found where I wrote the assignment.

"Can you just take a picture?" Joan asked, leaning across the table to pass me her phone.

I snapped a photo of the page and handed back her phone, our fingers brushing in the exchange.

"Thanks." She smiled at me, and I smiled back. My fingertips felt warm where they'd touched her skin. I wondered if maybe I could stop the hating her part of my brain and just like her.

Maybe.

After school, Ballard and I walked to the parking lot, passing Wade leaning on his silver Lexus. We gave him a wide berth, but just the sight of him made my insides churn.

Ballard still didn't want to ride so I pedaled toward the river alone. It wasn't as good as kissing, but biking did keep my tics mildly under control.

I was halfway across the Tallapoosa Bridge when I spotted Joan behind the wheel of her pink Volkswagen Beetle. The car was way too cheerful for her, with its painted-on eyelashes over the headlights and a Ping-Pong ball happy face bobbing on the antenna.

I dropped my feet to the concrete and watched her go past, her hands gripping the wheel so tight I could see the tension from a mile away.

Probably mad at Wade, I thought bitterly.

Wade was why I mostly avoided Joan. Back in middle school, she tried real hard to be my friend. One day, as

Wade dragged me down the hall, doing his rendition of "If I Only Had a Brain" while I tried not to fall on my face, Joan appeared in front of us. She stood there until we reached her, and then she punched Wade in the nose.

For a while after the punch, Wade didn't mess with me. His friends, however, did. They laughed when I passed their lockers. No one ever said a word about Wade getting punched. Wade was too popular, too good on the football field, his dad too high up in Moorhen's biggest job-providing company, TeleCell. Instead of ribbing Wade for getting beat up by a girl, they turned it back on me.

"Stephen Luckie," one of his friends had said, "needs a girl to be his bodyguard."

I watched Joan drive past with my stomach in knots. It had never made sense to me, after she punched him, how she could date him, but by our freshman year, when Wade was a sophomore, he and Joan were always together.

I remember being a little kid and being told that if a girl was mean to me it meant she liked me. I didn't think that was true, and even though Joan did eventually end up dating Wade, it seemed too easy an answer.

As the pink Volkswagen disappeared into town, I raised my middle finger in a halfhearted gesture. Hey, Joan, why defend me against Wade and then suck face with the 007-quoting bastard?

I lowered my middle finger as a car slowed to a stop beside me.

"Son," Dad said from behind the wheel of his maroon Camry. He wore the disappointed expression I knew so well, his dark brows thick frowns on his forehead.

"Father," I said, ever the smart-ass.

Dad spoke through gritted teeth. "I saw that profane gesture you just made. I will meet you at the house. No lollygagging. Ride straight home."

My foot jerked. My shoulder did this fast rise-and-fall thing three times in a row. That was new. Dad pretended not to notice. I pretended not to notice. For a moment, we both stared at each other, pretending not to notice.

"Yes, sir." He wasn't going to go away until he got the respectful reply he was waiting for.

He drove off and I turned to follow him, resisting the urge to use my middle finger one more time.

Dad was already at the kitchen table by the time I put my bike in the garage and left my sneakers by the door. He had a cup of black coffee—he only drinks black coffee—and his mouth looked like maybe my grimace tic was contagious.

"Sorry," I said, automatically. But *sorry* never worked on Dad.

"I'm disappointed in you, Stephen."

"You always are," I said.

Note to self: In the future, at least attempt to look contrite. Don't poke the bear.

"Why would you think that was okay?" He couldn't lecture me like a normal father. No, he had to make me give my own lecture, doing all the work for both of us.

I sighed. "It's not okay. I know now. Your stellar parenting skills enlightened me."

"What if a church member had driven past? Is this the

image you want them to have of their pastor's son?" His fingers drummed the side of his coffee cup.

Honestly, I never considered church members' opinions. Back in Auburn, Mom served a small traditional church, and it was obvious people paid attention to me. In third grade, as my whole family adjusted to my shiny new Tourette's diagnosis, members of the congregation took turns bringing us supper and patting my head sympathetically, hugging Mom, shaking Dad's hand. It was like I'd died and stuck around to witness the funeral. Hello people, neurodivergence is not a death sentence. It made me feel totally messed up, even though I wasn't.

But our church in Moorhen, The Exchange, was different. I tried to imagine our youth minister, Matt, freaking out over my gesture toward Joan's car. He wouldn't though.

The door opened behind me and Mom bustled in, dropping a Bible and notebook on the table as she kicked off her shoes. "What's up with my two favorite men?"

I groaned and dropped into a chair.

"I caught your son flipping someone the bird on the Tallapoosa Bridge." Dad spoke to Mom but kept his eyes on me.

When I was in trouble, that's how he referred to me. "Your son." Dad never wanted to claim me when I wasn't holding an honor roll certificate or working on a science fair project.

"Stephen?" Her eyes darted from me to Dad and back again.

"It was stupid." My shoulder did the three quick shrugs of the new tic. Crap. They'd been getting better. "I was mad at this girl, and no one was around, so I flipped her off. She was long gone. She didn't see. Only Dad saw."

"Well, it's not a gesture I'm particularly fond of." Mom sat across from me. "What girl was this?"

"It doesn't matter." I stared at my hands, the fingers flexing lightly, not as dramatic as the night of the party, walking up the stairs behind Sylvie.

"It must matter, if it was worth the angry gesture."

"It doesn't. Really. It was a stupid impulse and I won't do it again."

Mom sighed and glanced at her phone, which was lying faceup on the table. Her heart wasn't in this lecture, and I knew it.

Dad knew it too, because he chose that moment to slurp the last of his coffee and cross the kitchen to the sink. "Spaghetti sound good to everyone?"

"Spaghetti sounds great," Mom told him, scooping up her phone.

"Sure," I said, grateful for the change of topic and anxious to get out of the room. I wasn't myself right then, and I needed to clear my head.

"Oliver Rohn's in the hospital," Mom said, tapping out a text. "I need to go up there after dinner."

Dad nodded and turned on the faucet to fill a pot with water to boil. "His heart again?"

I used their distraction to escape the kitchen. I'd have to find some way to work out everything inside my head. Even if Sylvie didn't need me to protect her, I still had a scribbled-marker feeling in my brain, like someone had attacked my thoughts with a Sharpie.

With the door closed and my parents' voices muffled, I pulled out my guitar and fiddled with the strings. I'd taught myself to play over the summer.

Stashed under my bed was a notebook I'd snatched from Mom's collection. She had so many blank spirals and book-bound journals, she'd never notice one missing. It had a soft, floppy cover made of a thin wood grain. So far, it only held a few scribbled lines, ideas that might become songs, if I could ever make the melodies work.

Quietly, I strummed and sang, "Be still, myself, the kiss will overcome . . ." A blatant rip-off of a hymn we sang in church. Maybe if I started by rewording tunes I already knew, it would be easier to come up with my own later.

Unfortunately, I mentioned this to my mother and she mentioned it to Matt, the youth minister at The Exchange, and he started bugging me to play in the youth band. At least he hadn't gotten Brian, the worship pastor, in on the plan yet.

There was a knock on my bedroom door. I stilled my fingers, and there went the shoulder again. Jump. Jump. Jump. Always three times. Shit. That tic was gonna stick around a while. Exactly what I needed.

"Yeah," I called out.

"It's me," Mom said.

"Come in." I lowered the guitar to my lap and flipped the thin green pick from finger to finger.

Mom poked her head in the door. "You okay?"

"Sure." I nodded. "I'm great."

"You took your dad by surprise." She stepped inside and

leaned against the doorjamb. "He worries you're going to act a fool and get me in trouble, but that's just the past hanging over him. It's nothing to do with you."

I knew she was right. Mom worked at a tiny church south of Montgomery right out of seminary. She and Dad were dating, and the congregation was incredibly conservative. The Conference never should've appointed a woman there. Dad was busily making a name for himself in the world of science, and he published an article on evolution and the Bible, which landed in a church member's hands.

Mom was reappointed.

Dad knew our actions could affect my mother's job. What never sank in was this: Mom didn't care.

"Anyway," Mom said. "If you want to talk about this girl, about whatever made you angry—"

"It's really nothing," I said.

I used to get angry a lot, and I knew she got anxious when my temper showed, but the thing on the bridge really wasn't a big deal. She didn't need to worry.

"Okay then. I'm heading back to the hospital. You need anything while I'm out?"

I shook my head. "Thanks though."

After Mom left, I stared at the pick in my hand, moving it between my fingers and reliving the moment on the bridge when I saw Joan's face, how she looked pissed, and I felt pissed, and I realized I had no right to be upset over Joan still liking Wade.

Middle school was ancient history. I really needed to let go of my Joan obsession and focus on other girls, girls I might actually have a chance with, especially if Ballard's experiment somehow worked and I could gain control over my tics.

That was a catch-22 though. I needed a girl to like me before she would kiss me, and the tics didn't stop until the kissing started. I didn't think even Ballard could find a solution to that problem.

Chapter Four

The next day was Friday, and Ballard was going to the Moorhen football game, but I wasn't up to faking interest in which way some jocks were running on a field. I'd spent way too much time dodging the guys on the team, ignoring the way they jerked their bodies to mimic mine. I just couldn't cheer for them.

I'd convinced Mom to drive me into Auburn for a trip to the bike shop. She'd gotten excited and started planning a whole evening.

"Yo, Luckie," Ballard called as I unlocked my bike after school. I used two separate bike locks, because the idea of someone stealing her sent shivers of panic down my spine. My bike's an authentic 1956 Schwinn Hornet. I call her Gwinn the Schwinn.

"Yeah?" I glanced back over one shoulder, and it jerked hard. Three times. So, basically, I slammed my own shoulder into my own chin and knocked my own teeth together so hard tears sprang to my eyes.

"Stay at my place tomorrow night? At the lake?" Ballard leaned against his car, backpack at his Chaco-clad feet.

"Probably not," I said, shaking away the pain. "You know I gotta be home for church on Sunday."

"Just ask. And ask the right reverend, not the mad scientist. It's important."

"How so?" I pushed my kickstand up with one foot, balancing with the other, and rolled backward until I was closer to him.

"The experiment, bro. The experiment." Ballard widened his eyes and nodded, like he was speaking in code. I guess he sort of was, but at the moment, it wasn't my dad that came off as the crazy one.

A quick look around the parking lot revealed no one watching us. "It's never gonna work, Ballard. Forget it."

"I have a real plan now. We're golden."

"What's the plan?" My fingers flexed on the handlebars. If there was one thing I'd learned from Ballard's past schemes, it's that he was always golden, but I never was.

"Not now. Someone might hear." His eyes darted left to right.

I doubted anyone cared, but he was right. School wasn't the place to discuss a kissing experiment. "Fine, I'll ask, but I can't promise anything."

With a grin and a fist bump, Ballard hopped into his Jeep, swinging his backpack in behind him. I put my feet on the pedals and rode out of the parking lot.

Halfway home, I spotted Mom driving toward me in her green Mazda, almost the same shade as my Schwinn. She pulled over and secured Gwinn in the bike rack while I tossed my book bag into the backseat.

"Good day?" Mom asked once she was behind the wheel again.

I shrugged and turned on the radio, scanning for the local rock station.

"Math test go okay?" Mom watched me from the corner of her eye.

"Just a quiz," I told her. "No big deal; we're only a week into school."

She went on asking questions about my classes. She always knows everything thanks to a program the school uses. She can access my homework assignments, exam schedule, etc.

"Well, I'm glad school is off to a good start." Mom smiled. "And I'm glad we're doing this."

"Me too," I said. "It's been a while."

"It has been a while," she said.

We used to do stuff all the time. When Mom had to travel to speak about the process of starting a new church, I'd go with her and find a good trail to ride, but she hadn't taken many speaking engagements in the last year. The Exchange was growing fast and took up more and more of her time.

Dad spent a lot of time with me when I was in the ten and under category. Back then, he and I got each other. Back then, it was the coolest thing ever to pull out my *Gross Kitchen Science* book and spend an afternoon making things bubble and stink with my father.

My mom and I rode in silence for a while, and then I mentioned our reading list for the semester, including *The Crucible* and *The Great Gatsby*. I knew Mom would be thrilled about *The Great Gatsby*.

"Oh, we can rent the movie," Mom almost squealed with delight. "Both of them. Robert and Leo, all in one night."

I rolled my eyes. "Sure, sounds fun."

By the time we pulled up to the bike shop, Mom had told me all about their 1920s themed prom from her high school days and had me check if the movies were streaming anywhere.

We entered the shop and the bell overhead tinkled. At the cash register, a cute girl I didn't recognize looked up. She smiled at me, and I smiled back. Allen must have hired her to replace the kid who used to work the front. He'd probably graduated and moved on. As I rolled my bike through the store, I thought about all the reasons I could visit the bike shop and get to know the new girl. She'd smiled at me and then dropped her eyes in that coy way girls sometimes do, sort of shy-like. Maybe I could get up the guts to talk to her when I picked my bike up. I'd have to convince Mom to wait in the car.

Allen met me in the back with a broad smile on his bony face.

"How's Gwinn?" He gave me and the Schwinn a once-over.

"Gorgeous as ever," I told him, concentrating hard to suppress a shoulder twitch. "But I've got an issue with one of the bolts."

While Allen and I talked bike maintenance, Mom browsed the cycling gear, though I'm sure she didn't have a clue what any of it was. I used to try to get her to ride with me, but neither of my parents were fond of the outdoors. Dad prefers books and computer screens, and Mom would rather be watching old movies with a glass of wine.

Allen rolled Gwinn out to the little garage in back and I turned to look for Mom, but she was gone.

I scanned the racks, fighting a quake in my gut. My fingers flexed and the tension built in my shoulder. I'd held it off too long. It was about to . . . jerkjerkjerk. There it went, extra hard after holding it back. Still no sign of Mom. Sweat beaded my forehead and suddenly I felt like I was seven again, lost and scared in a crowd. Sometimes my emotional reactions are more intense than the situation calls for, but knowing that never makes them stop.

I took another step toward the door, hoping Mom went outside to take a phone call, and the cashier called out, "Excuse me."

I turned to her, my face already twisting into a grimace. Her attention made things worse. I'd really hoped to talk to her later, not fall apart in front of her within ten minutes of meeting. The tension built and then . . . shoulder jerk, face grimace, finger flex, foot fling.

The cashier was lifting her phone from the cradle as she spoke. "Are you okay? Do I need to call someone?"

She was so pretty, dark hair in a messy bun and eyes full of concern.

"Like, should I call 911?" She leaned forward on the counter, still holding the phone.

"No," I snapped, fighting to control the grimace. If I could at least keep my face normal, that'd be great. "I'm fine. I have Tourette's."

For years, I wouldn't tell anyone about Tourette's syndrome. If a stranger asked, I'd stare wide-eyed until Mom came to the rescue or else I'd flat-out run away.

Eventually, I discovered it's easier to own it. It is what it is, and there's even a lot of good to be said for neurodivergence. Mom says that most of the historic figures that changed our world for the better were probably neurodivergent. Their brains worked differently, so they thought differently, and then they acted differently, and it made a difference. However, if I could just lose the tics themselves, then maybe a girl would notice me for some reason other than to be scared something was wrong with me.

"Oh." She lowered the phone. "That's the one where you curse a lot, right?"

My cheeks burned and my whole body ached with the effort of holding back tics.

"Like on that show? I can't remember the name, but it was on MTV, and the kid would scream out curse words . . ." She trailed off, watching me.

"No," I said through gritted teeth.

Now it was her turn to blush. "I'm sorry. I just—"

I cut her off. "It's fine."

But it wasn't fine. I was out of time and the tics won. Jerk jerk jerk went my shoulder. I covered my face to hide my grimace.

The bell over the door tinkled and Mom reappeared with two lemonades. "I couldn't resist popping over to Toomer's. Here." She handed me one cup, smiling like a kid with cotton candy.

"I'm really sorry," the cashier said again.

Mom's smile faded as she watched my face.

"Can we go now?" I asked. "Let's go for a walk or something. Allen can call when Gwinn's ready."

"Sure," Mom answered, looking from me to the pretty girl who no longer tempted me at all.

Mom didn't need to ask what was wrong after we left the store. She squeezed my shoulder once, an unspoken apology, and changed the subject. "Let's walk to The Gnu's Room. Maybe we can find a copy of *Gatsby*."

I glanced over my shoulder toward the bike shop, a glare on the front window blocking my view of the cashier. Mom was already crossing the street, so I jogged to catch up.

I followed her down the sidewalk, sipping my lemonade, willing myself to let go of the frustration. All of my muscles were coiled, snakes full of hissing anger. The scene in the bike shop would make Mom sympathetic when I asked for a Sunday off from church. A weekend at Lake Martin could be what I needed to relax and ease my anxiety. Maybe I should thank the clueless cashier after all.

Maybe, but really no. Even if it did gain my mother's sympathy and get me what I wanted, it sucked. Plain and simple. I'd have to pass the girl again when I went back to get my bike later, and she'd look at me with pity. I didn't want anybody's pity.

Dinner was mostly good. We went to Venditori's, my favorite from when we lived there. Mom was chatty, so she filled the time before our orders arrived with news of church members and relatives.

I tried to look attentive while working to put the bike shop cashier behind me, folding and unfolding my napkin.

When our food came, Mom said grace, and I talked while buttering a breadstick. "So, you know how stress makes my tics worse?"

"I do." Mom swirled her spaghetti and held my gaze.

"Well, going back to school has me anxious, and the tics are pretty bad."

"I noticed a few new ones this week," Mom said.

"Yeah, my shoulder has been jerking, and my foot. It's exhausting." I put down the butter knife and took a bite of the bread.

"Is there anything we can do?" Mom asked.

We'd tried all sorts of things over the years. Some of it helped. I visited a chiropractor and Mom kept me well stocked in supplements. But I didn't want another doctor to visit or pill to swallow.

"I need to chill. I was considering heading to the lake tomorrow night, with Ballard. Maybe I can spend the night." I jabbed my ravioli with the fork and took a big bite. I registered tension in my shoulder and swallowed fast.

"Sounds like a good idea." Mom watched my shoulder jerk. "Is that what you were talking about?"

"Yeah. I rammed my own jaw this afternoon."

She frowned.

"It's okay, no big deal." I wiggled my chin to show her. "I just want to go sit on the back deck and watch the water, listen to the wind chimes. Breathe a bit, ya know?"

Mom loves a silent retreat, so I knew the image would appeal to her.

"Are you on the volunteer list for preschool journey groups Sunday morning?"

"Journey groups" is what Sunday School classes are called at The Exchange. Sometimes I volunteer with the little kids, though I am mostly just crowd control for the classroom.

"Nope, not my Sunday."

Mom mulled it over, chewing a bite of garlic bread and watching my face for signs of a lie.

I'm not a good liar, but what I'd said was close enough to truth that it passed muster. The tics were getting worse. I wanted to get away. And I *would* spend some time sitting on the deck watching the water. I always did when I visited Lake Martin.

Whatever Ballard had planned, I didn't know enough about it to make up a lie, and I was pretty sure it wouldn't work anyway.

"Okay. You can take my car. Be back for youth Sunday night." She reached across the table and snatched a cherry tomato from my salad bowl. "And no drinking."

I rolled my eyes. "I don't drink, Mom. My meds, remember?"

Of course she remembered, but she always reminded me anyway.

After dinner, we walked back to the bike shop. I breathed a sigh of relief when the cashier was already gone for the day. Allen was by himself, getting ready to lock up.

"Thanks," I told him, rolling Gwinn out the door while Mom went to get the car.

"No problem. I always love to work on that bike. Bring 'er in anytime." Allen gave a smile and a wave when Mom pulled up to the sidewalk.

While driving home, Mom took a call and agreed to meet the caller at The Exchange as soon as we made it back to Moorhen. The voice sounding from the speaker was feminine and a little bit hysterical. Mom sighed when she hung up. I knew she was looking forward to going home and relaxing. But her job meant being on call 24/7.

We pulled up at the old mall and parked near The Exchange entrance. There weren't any stores in the mall anymore, only our church, which took up the out-of-date movie theater and four retail spaces, and a few local law and medical offices. Mostly it was falling apart, trees sprouting through cracks in the asphalt and windows broken by bored kids.

I pulled Gwinn from the bike rack and promised Mom I'd ride straight home. It was only a mile, so I planned to circle the block a few times to clear my head.

The whole thing with the cashier was still eating at me, though I hadn't wanted to let Mom see how much it bothered me. How was I ever supposed to get a girlfriend if the female species saw me as someone in need of help? If I tried to kiss another girl, she'd call 911 and report a seizure.

But I wanted to kiss another girl.

As I turned out of the parking lot, an SUV turned in. Mom waited by the entrance, keys in hand. The driver looked familiar, and it only took two seconds for me to catch why.

We live in teeny tiny Moorhen, Alabama. There are only two Asian families among our ranks. The Itos lived on the edge of town, and Mr. Ito worked at the Toyota plant nearby. Then there were the Pearsons, Joan's family. Her dad was white, and her mother was Korean. I saw Mrs. Pearson in the halls every day at school.

It was Mrs. Pearson behind the wheel of the SUV pulling to a stop by my mother's Mazda. She stepped from the driver's seat and darted across the parking lot to meet Mom. She looked different out of context, her dark hair hanging around her face like Joan's, her button-down with slacks uniform replaced by green yoga pants and a big T-shirt. She looked young, like a regular person more than a teacher.

I rode home with my mind on Mrs. Pearson's presence at our church. I'd never seen any of her family there before. They weren't members. And she was upset on the phone with my mother. How did she even know my mother? And why did I care?

I knew the answer. I cared because of Joan, but Joan barely noticed my existence.

By the time I closed the garage and went inside, I'd made a decision. Whatever ridiculous plan Ballard had concocted, I was going to do it. Maybe if I got my tics under control, Joan would notice more than my existence.

Chapter Five

I stayed up late playing *Call of Duty* and toying with my guitar. Mom came home well after midnight. Whatever Mrs. Pearson needed to talk about, it sure was a long talk. I almost asked Mom what was going on there, but I knew she wouldn't break Mrs. Pearson's confidence just to help me better understand Joan.

By the time I woke up on Saturday, noon had come and gone. I showered, dressed, and grabbed a pack of Pop-Tarts on my way out the door.

Dad was shut up in his makeshift office. I could hear him talking in the slow, deliberate way he does when he's dictating. He says he writes better out loud, but his typing is almost as loud as his talking.

Mom was nowhere to be found, but she'd remembered to take Dad's car. I snagged her keys from the hook in the kitchen and shouted a goodbye to Dad on my way out the door.

Ballard was waiting on the deck of the lake house when I arrived. He passed me a cold can of Coke and motioned for me to sit in one of the Adirondack chairs.

"I'm still not sure this experiment is a good idea," I told him, popping the tab.

"If you hate my plan, you can bail."

"Okay, so, what's your plan?" I asked.

"We're going to a party tonight." Ballard wore navy plaid pajama pants and a Moorhen High T-shirt. By the water, I spotted his mother and eleven-year-old sister, Blair, walking toward us.

"That's the big plan? A party?" The little bit of faith I had in Ballard finding girls willing to kiss me shriveled up and died.

"Not just any party," Ballard said. "The perfect party for this experiment."

"You know I'm always nervous at parties. I need to be relaxed if I'm going to kiss someone."

Footsteps sounded and Ballard looked up. "Hey, Mom, you look nice today."

Mrs. Keighley paused on the steps and frowned. "Compliments won't get you out of chores. Hop to."

With an it-was-worth-a-shot shrug, Ballard stood, and I followed him inside. There were windows everywhere on the side of the house facing the lake. I could see the shoreline and a handful of chimes hanging from tree limbs. My stomach clenched at the idea of a party tonight. I don't know what I thought Ballard would come up with, but going to a party did not constitute a plan.

"We're going out to lunch," his mom told us. "You boys want us to bring you something back?"

"That'd be great." Ballard smiled as he opened the dishwasher and loaded the cereal bowls. Around his parents, he was an angel. Perfect Southern gentleman, my mom called him. "Thanks for thinking of us."

"When you finish the dishes, sweep the downstairs, and then you're free." Mrs. Keighley took her purse from the counter, a green leather monstrosity, and nudged Blair forward. Blair waved at me as they left.

Once we were alone again, Ballard dropped the ultra-polite voice. "This party is a few doors down at my cousin Clara's place. Her parents will be over here with mine, and none of them give a shit what we get up to. So Clara invited a ton of kids from her school in Dadeville. I told her about the experiment."

"You what?" Tension pulsed in my shoulder muscles.

"Relax, Clara's cool. She won't say a word." Ballard dropped a handful of spoons into the dishwasher.

"I don't care how cool she is. That's private." My fingers flexed on the kitchen table.

"Listen, man. She said there would be a whole group of girls there with their own experiment going." His grin was contagious, and I had to smile.

"What's the experiment?" I asked, letting my faith in Ballard breathe again.

"Well, it's more like a group challenge. They're all seniors and have some sort of bucket list of high school experiences. Tonight, they're working on kissing strangers at a party."

"And?"

"And we need to make sure you are one of the strangers available at this party. No sex, ya know, only kissing. They've set up strict boundaries. That fits our experiment to a tee." He tossed a plastic bowl in the air, watching it spin before catching it with one hand and adding it to the dishwasher.

He was right. A whole lot of kissing-only girl encounters would give us some solid data to analyze. Not that data analysis was ever the real reason for this harebrained scheme.

"Okay." I nodded. "It's worth a shot. At least it's their idea, and they only want to kiss, right?"

"Yeah, at least this squad is honest about what they're up to. No gray areas."

The day passed slowly, filled with video games and the squealing laughter of Ballard's sister through the wall. She'd recruited their nine-year-old brother, Bryce, and convinced him to play beauty salon.

Even after the sun sank below the lake, the water shining like glass, we didn't leave the house. Only clueless nerds show up to a party before nine. Or so Ballard said.

We snagged two burgers off the grill while Mr. Keighley added more.

Ballard's aunt and uncle arrived, and the women mixed drinks while the men talked football. The Keighleys were Auburn fans, like my family, but the other couple rooted for Alabama. It'd been a good day for both teams, so everyone was in a good mood and they were drinking happily as they rehashed the day's games.

By the time Ballard and I left them behind, everyone was tipsy and the little kids were conked out upstairs. It was so different from how my family get-togethers played out, where no one ever drank more than a glass of wine and the talk often turned to scientific or theological theory by the time we got to dessert.

I envied Ballard sometimes. I couldn't picture my own father talking football with anyone. Maybe if he'd been that kind of dad I would know something about sports. Maybe we'd have something to talk about.

"While you're busy with the experiment, I've got a quest of my own." Ballard walked backward along the trail, reaching up to grab tree limbs.

"A quest?"

"The perfect prom date." He grinned. "I figure if I make a good choice by Christmas, I have time to work at the relationship."

"Seriously?" I'd never heard Ballard talk about a relationship with any girl. He was all about the hookup. Or the minor hookup, at least. He'd never closed the deal.

He wasn't grinning anymore. He was dead serious. "Absolutely. That's the key. If I can get the girl to fall in love with me, sex on prom night is pretty much a guarantee."

"Ballard, that's not how it works."

"It might. I refuse to leave junior year still a damn virgin, and I don't want to have sex just to have sex. I want to actually like the girl, have a real relationship, ya know?"

I was surprised to hear Ballard talk like that, but also glad. It was about time he quit jumping from girl to girl. It was also weird to be going to a party where I planned to kiss strangers and Ballard planned to look for a serious relationship.

He turned to walk frontways, and we didn't say much else until the party house loomed before us. Twinkle lights lined the dock, and a bunch of kids sat with their feet in the water and beers in their hands.

Clara's parents, the Jordans, had bought three lots to build on, ensuring there'd be no other houses within throwing distance. The windows glowed yellow, and Lizzo boomed from the speakers. A girl in a neon tube top waved from the railing, where she balanced on high heels, one hand gripping a tree branch.

"She's going to fall," I said.

But she didn't. Instead, some guy in a Dadeville football jersey scooped her into his arms and carried her away giggling.

"I so didn't invite her," a voice behind us said.

I turned around to meet Clara, Ballard's cousin. She shared Ballard's red locks, but not much else. No freckles and no easygoing smile.

"Hey, cuz." Ballard gave her a hug. "Direct us to the drinks."

"In the kitchen, obviously." She pointed toward the house. She turned to me. "You must be Stephen. You don't look like anything's wrong with you."

As if on cue, my shoulder jerked.

"Did you do that on purpose?" Clara asked. "'Cause if you're making this Tourette's shit up to get girls, that's pretty sick."

"Relax, Clara." Ballard put an arm around her and started up the steps. "I've known Stephen since middle school. Trust me. He's got Tourette's."

I crossed my arms and shifted my weight from one foot to the other. I couldn't believe any girl thought Tourette's would work as a pickup strategy. I didn't want some kind of pity-based relationship.

I followed them up the stairs, fingers flexing in my jeans pockets. I'd expected my tics to be worse tonight, what with the anxiety caused by Ballard's plan. Instead, I was excited and strangely calm. The only time the tics got out of control was when I got stuck on how to get these girls to kiss me. I mean, was I supposed to walk up to a random girl and say, "Excuse me, are you one of the girls trying to kiss strangers?"

"Anyway," Clara said as she opened the door to the kitchen and we went inside, "these girls are all pretty confident. If they choose you, they choose you. They won't play games or act shy or anything."

I rubbed my shoulder to suppress a jerk.

"Keep your hands to yourselves if you know what's good for you. I won't have any guy being creepy at my party."

"Yes ma'am," Ballard said with a mock salute.

"The whole thing is ridiculous if you ask me," Clara continued. "But no one asked me, so whatev. You boys can take care of yourselves now. I need to make the rounds."

We watched Clara saunter back out the door, her tall frame and thin heels giving her an air of authority.

"Her mother's an event planner," Ballard told me. "She takes party hostessing very seriously."

"Now what?" I asked, my nerves reminding me they didn't like new situations.

"I'm off to find a potential prom date, and you are off to look casual and cool so a few of these girls might notice you." Ballard grabbed a brown bottle from a cooler on the floor and saluted me with one hand. "Hope you get lucky, bro."

I groaned. "Quit with the lucky stuff. It got old five years ago."

His face stilled, his eyes losing the playful twinkle of his party-king persona. "Seriously, man, try to have fun tonight, and text if you need me. We can leave anytime you want."

I nodded.

Ballard crossed his fingers and smiled at me. "Good luck."

After Ballard disappeared into the crowd, I wandered out of the kitchen and glanced from group to group. Three girls held court by the fireplace, all of them beautiful. One wore a white tank top, bright against her dark skin. One had on a pink sundress covered in polka dots, and the other girl wore a blue Dadeville High T-shirt.

I had no way of knowing if these girls were part of the kissing group, but the way they were casing the room made me think it was possible. The girl in the sundress caught my eye and smiled. Her hair was pitch-black, and she sort of reminded me of Joan.

For a moment, I was a typical high school guy at a party, a guy about to meet a girl he might like.

Then I remembered that I was still me and had no idea how to talk to half the girls I knew, let alone a girl I just met.

As the girl in the pink dress leaned forward, a hairbreadth from a step in my direction, I did a 180 and left the room.

The hallway was packed as I wove my way through into a game room full of even more people. I froze there, not sure what to do next.

As I considered texting Ballard to call the whole thing off, someone grabbed my arm. "Hey, don't I know you?"

I jumped, my heart pounding over the music. "Me?"

"Yeah, I swear I know you from somewhere. You don't go to Dadeville, do you? I haven't seen you there." She had long brown hair. And I mean super long, like past her waist. I'd never seen hair so long before.

"I go to Moorhen," I said, steeling my spine against a twitch. "I don't think we know each other."

She ran a hand through her wicked long hair and examined my face. "Have you always lived in Moorhen?"

I hid my flexing fingers behind my back while I explained, "I was in Auburn until seventh grade."

She grinned, and her teeth were slightly crooked. I found them attractive. My shoulder jerked and I desperately hoped she hadn't noticed.

"That's it. I remember now. Your mom is Reverend Luckie, right? You were in my Sunday School class."

I flushed guiltily over not remembering her, but Mom served a few churches in the Auburn area over the years, and there's no way I could remember all those people. "That's her. She's at The Exchange in Moorhen now. It's pretty cool, The Exchange."

I stopped talking. Rambling about my mother and church was not the way to snag a girl. The girls in the living room had panicked me, but I forgot about the experiment so long as this girl looked at me.

"I'm Pilar," she said. "It's fine if you don't remember me. No worries."

"I'm sorry," I said. "It's just been a long time."

"You'll remember me from now on though, right?" She raised a perfect eyebrow.

"Of course." I blushed, though I couldn't tell you why. What she said felt suggestive in some way. The only girl I'd spent much time around was Erin, and Erin's words never affected the parts of me Pilar's words affected.

I wasn't sure what to say, but I wanted to keep talking to Pilar. The best I could come up with was, "How've you been?"

Someone turned the volume up, and my words were overrun by the loud, fast beat.

"What?" She leaned closer.

"I said, how've you been?" I was practically yelling my inane question. I felt silly.

"Let's go somewhere quiet." She motioned to the speaker in the corner and turned to walk down the hallway.

This wasn't like following Sylvie upstairs. Then I knew what was going to happen, at least to some extent. It was a kissing game. We were going to kiss. Following Pilar was different. My heart was more bass than the sounds of Khalid blaring behind us, and I had no idea what would happen next.

She led me to a room with only a few people inside. A couple was sprawled across the couch, only half dressed, and a group of boys huddled around their phones laughing at TikTok videos. There was a loveseat in one corner and we dropped onto the cushions. As we sat, my shoulder jerked three times. I glanced at Pilar.

"You okay?" she asked, concern creasing her forehead.

"Yeah, I'm fine, it's just—"

"In Sunday School, you used to make machine-gun noises." She cocked her head to one side. "It drove the teacher crazy. Papá said you couldn't help it."

I squirmed in the seat, not wanting this conversation to

be about Tourette's. In general, I don't mind having Tourette's, but it's a pain to explain to other people. They only know the stereotypes, and I get tired of being everyone's neurodivergence educator.

"I made the machine-gun sounds to cover the throat clearing. It's called Tourette's. Shooting noises seemed cooler than throat clearing."

She nodded like she truly got it. "It's cool. Everyone's got struggles, right?"

I leaned closer to hear her better.

"Like my little brother. He has ADHD. He takes meds and stuff. He thinks really differently than I do. Plus, he's smart and fun. I bet you are too."

"Thanks," I said, and maybe it was true. I could be smart and fun, because Pilar said so. Something about how she talked, how she carried herself, told me she wasn't a girl anyone said no to.

"Do you like it in Moorhen?" she asked.

"I like my friends here, and I like our church better, but I miss Auburn. We go back pretty often. They have way cooler events and restaurants and stuff with the university and all. Do you go back a lot?"

"No, my parents are super strict. I barely leave the house except for school and church. It's mostly okay, though. I'm not much of a party person. My cousin made me come to this one." Pilar twisted so she was facing me, one leg pressed against the back of the loveseat. "I had to convince my mom Isabel was helping me study for the ACT."

"Parties stress me out," I told her. "My best friend, Ballard, convinced me to come with him to this one."

“I’m glad you came.” She leaned forward an inch or so.

I willed my shoulder not to jerk and said, “I’m glad I came too.

“I’ve never done this,” I added. “I mean, met a girl at a party.”

Pilar smiled and moved closer, tucking herself against me. We could hear each other better that way, and it felt comfortable, how she fit snug and warm.

“I haven’t done this either,” Pilar said. “But if you think about it, it’s not like we’re total strangers. We’ve known each other for years. Sort of.”

I nodded, my chin resting on her head. “True. And we met at church, of all places. Very proper.”

She laughed and pulled her head back so she could look at me. I smiled.

“Very proper,” she repeated.

Then she kissed me.

I wasn’t expecting her to kiss me. The experiment had flown right out of my head. But, every centimeter of my skin sparked like electricity. I kissed her back, my fingers in her curtain of hair.

“Pilar,” a girl called from the door.

She pulled back from our kiss, and I smiled at her. She was smiling too before she glanced at the girl.

“Your mom called my mom. We’re busted.”

“Shit.” Pilar hopped up from the chair and handed me her cell phone. “Here, put your number in.”

“Pilar, the longer we wait, the worse this will get,” the girl said.

“Isabel,” Pilar said, drawing the name out, “we’re already busted. Three extra seconds won’t change anything.”

Hurrying, I tapped the digits and hit save.

She slid the phone into her pocket, kissed my cheek, and left the room, followed by an impatient Isabel.

For a while, I sat on the loveseat, the cushion beside me still warm where Pilar had been. I pulled out my phone and had a text from Ballard.

Any luck?

That brought the experiment back to mind and I wondered if Pilar might have been one of the kissing girls after all. I didn't think so though. She didn't seem to be here with any group, just her cousin.

I believed she kissed me because she wanted to kiss me. Me, Stephen Luckie, not me, stranger at a party.

I texted Ballard back, *Sort of.*

When I looked around, the hookup couple and the video boys had disappeared. The three girls from the living room were on the couch, talking quietly.

The girl in the pink dress glanced around and saw me staring. When she got up to cross the room, my gut twisted. I'd kissed a girl, and I'd been right. Not a single tic while I kissed her, but it was a short kiss. And the whole point of this party was to kiss multiple girls, not just one.

True scientific experiments required gathering as much data as possible.

But Pilar hadn't been part of the experiment. At least, I hadn't kissed her to gather data. I would've been happy to kiss her with no experiment at all.

The girl dropped onto the loveseat beside me. "Was that your girlfriend who just left?"

I shook my head. My fingers flexed, but she never looked down.

"What's your name?"

"Stephen." I considered getting up, pushing her away, calling the whole thing quits.

But I didn't.

Up close, this girl wasn't so intimidating. Her eyes were a light brown color behind her silver-rimmed glasses, and she even seemed a bit nervous now that she was this close.

"I'd like to kiss you," she said. Very matter-of-fact.

And okay, yeah, I liked Pilar, but I'd just met her, fourth grade Sunday School notwithstanding. And this girl was practically in my lap, asking me to kiss her. If I'd walked away, Ballard would've never let me live it down.

I leaned in, pushing my lips tentatively against her mouth. Her lips were slightly dry, and she didn't push for anything more than one quick kiss.

"Thank you," she said after. "We're doing this high school bucket list thing."

I nodded. "I heard about it. From Clara."

"Really? So you know it's just kissing, then?" The girl in the T-shirt walked over.

"Right," I answered.

"This will sound weird, but can we kiss you too? We want to knock it off the list, but when we tried to kiss a couple of other guys tonight, they were assholes about it."

My fingers flexed and I rearranged my hands to hide the movement. "I guess. I mean, sure. Yeah."

I should've at least asked for the girls' names, but the

whole thing felt too good to be true in the moment. The girl in the white tank top grabbed my hand and pulled me to my feet. She was really short, like barely five feet, and I had to bend over to give her a peck on the lips. Then she and the first girl moved aside so I could kiss the girl in the T-shirt.

She was a little more aggressive, with a dagger of a tongue, but I wasn't as into it as I thought I would be anyhow. Kissing those girls felt hollow. They were all pretty and seemed nice enough, but I didn't know them. Regardless of my lack of mental involvement, other parts of me did rise to the occasion. Was that how girls felt when guys like Wade moved so fast? I was flattered and willing, but also confused and ready to stop.

Thinking of Wade made me think of Joan for the second time that night. I wondered what she'd think about this experiment and felt embarrassed. I was glad the bucket list girls moved on quickly, leaving me to sort my own thoughts.

Walking home with a drunk Ballard at two o'clock in the morning, I tried to figure out if I'd had the best night of my life or the worst. It was exactly what I went there for, and the tics stopped, but Pilar threw a wrench in things. I wasn't sure I *liked* her liked her, but kissing her had been sweet and fun and it made the randomness of the other kisses all wrong.

Was sweet and fun conversation what it meant to like a girl? The only thing I had to compare it to was my fascination with Joan, but we'd hardly had a real conversation in the years of going to school together. How do people know when their feelings are more than physical?

"How many girls did you kiss?" Ballard asked.

"Three," I answered. Then I decided Pilar counted, even if it was different with her. "Well, four."

"And the tics?"

I shook my head. "None."

This was really good news. It meant some of my fears about relationships and sex could be let go. My body did have the ability to focus when it needed to.

And Pilar had been interested even though she knew I had Tourette's. That was even better than stopping my tics, the feeling of being wanted for who I am.

"Sweet." He grinned. "I bet my cousin knows of more parties next weekend."

"I'm done," I said. "I don't want to be one of those jerky guys who uses girls without even knowing their names."

"Stephen, you weren't using those girls any more than they were using you. No one got hurt, so what's the big deal?"

"I dunno," I said. "But it doesn't feel good."

"All four were bad kissers?"

"No. I mean, one was, sort of, but . . ." He wasn't going to get it, not while he was drunk. "Let's drop it, okay?"

We reached Ballard's house and made our way up the stairs. He was snoring as soon as his head hit the pillow. I lay on the second twin bed, staring at the ceiling, analyzing my supposed data. All four girls had kissed differently. Who knew there were so many ways to move your mouth?

I was happy with the results, excited to know my relationship prospects weren't as bleak as I had feared, but there was still that gnawing feeling in my gut. I didn't want to be a guy who made out with four girls in one night.

Before I fell asleep, my mind was full of Pilar's forever long hair, the taste of Coke still cold on her tongue, and how she didn't care at all about my tics.

Then Joan flashed across my brain. I don't know why, but there she was inside my head. I pictured her dark hair sweeping over me as Pilar's had done.

I didn't sleep well at all.

Chapter Six

Mom stopped in my doorway Sunday evening. "How was the lake?"

I was strumming my guitar, regretting the shot of espresso I'd had at youth. It was sure to keep me up half the night. My notebook was open on the floor, and I'd scribbled some lines about ice cream girls and their strawberry lips. When I sang them, I sounded like a one-man boy band, so I crossed them out.

"It was good," I told my mother, not meeting her eyes. "I feel a lot better now, a lot calmer."

She bit her lip, standing in my doorway. It was clear I'd lied, because my tics were still intense. I know she saw me at church, shoulder jerking and leg kicking at the same damn time. But she didn't push it, and I didn't want to talk. At least, not to my mother. Dad started typing and Mom glanced at the wall between us and his closet of an office.

"More edits?" I asked.

She nodded. And that was that. She went back to the living room, and I tried to make the idea of ice cream girls sound deep and soulful instead of poppy and bubble-gummy. It didn't happen. What did happen was I stayed awake until 3:00 a.m., hopped up on caffeine, rewriting the same sucky stanza over and over and over.

The next day, I was exhausted, and school was the last place I wanted to be. School was the last place I wanted to be every day, though, so I guess it wasn't much different than usual. I slept on my desk through most of study hall and was better by the time I sat down for lunch.

"Clara says she talked to those girls about you. Did you really make out with three of them at the same time?" Ballard asked through a mouthful of French fries.

Guilt churned in my gut again. "No, not at the same time. But yes, I kissed three of them. I told you this already."

Ballard stared in disbelief. "I was drunk, dude. I barely remember walking home, so I sure don't remember you telling me you made out with three different girls."

"Lower your voice." My eyes darted around the crowded cafeteria. It was a small room, requiring us to go to lunch in two shifts. I paused at the sight of Joan a few tables away, staring at me with an odd look on her face. "If you can't remember walking home, that's a problem. How is that even fun, drinking so much you can't remember anything?"

"I don't usually get that drunk, okay. And I wasn't driving. Plus, I had you there to get me home. I'm not a total idiot." He waved a French fry at me, lecturing. "Anyway, Clara also said you hooked up with some other girl, Pillar or something."

"Not pillar," I corrected him. "Pilar, like Pee-lar. And we didn't hook up. We talked."

"And kissed." Ballard smirked.

"And kissed," I conceded. "But only once, and not as part of the experiment. I . . . I like her."

“Did you get her digits?” He quit waving the fry and popped it into his mouth.

“No, but she has mine.” I sipped my carton of chocolate milk.

He laughed and smashed another handful of fries into his mouth, leaving a ring of grease around his lips. “That means she’s in control, so she can choose to not call you now.”

“It wasn’t like that,” I said, remembering her effortless confidence. “My phone was in my pocket and hers was out, so . . . never mind. It doesn’t matter. By now, she’s probably heard I kissed those other girls and written me off as a total jerk. Which I am.”

“You’re not a jerk. You are the least jerky person I know.” He paused and studied my face, which was twisted into a grimace as usual. “Unless you count the fact that your body parts jerk a lot. But that’s a whole other situation.”

Ballard could get away with joking about my tics. I chuckled, but wasn’t in the mood to truly laugh.

“You seriously feel bad, don’t you? You went from never kissing a girl to kissing four in one night and you feel *bad*. He shook his head slowly. “You must really like this Pilar.”

“She was easy to talk to. Girls are never easy to talk to.”

“Sure they are. You’re the one who makes it difficult, assuming they care about the Tourette’s. I promise, you think about that crap way more than the rest of us. I bet most girls at Moorhen don’t notice your tics anymore.”

I couldn’t believe he was even close to right, that no one noticed my tics anymore. Still there was a small nudge of truth in what he said. Was I the one to make it difficult?

I tried to remember the last time I attempted to talk to a girl, not including Erin, who was practically family. It must have been freshman year. Ballard dragged me to a football game and disappeared under the bleachers with one of his many girlfriends. I was left with her best friend, a quiet girl in pink-framed glasses who moved away a few months later. I stuttered over everything I said. I had a vocal tic, and it made my words come out like a scratched CD sometimes. Plus I was nervous as hell, and she was wearing the shortest shorts I'd ever seen.

We hadn't hit it off or ever talked again. I chalked it up to the Tourette's, the way my foot kept bouncing involuntarily on the metal benches. But maybe that wasn't the case. Maybe we didn't hit it off because we didn't hit it off.

My stomach flipped at this, that I could be looking at everything through the lens of my differences, judging girls for judging me without even knowing them. I couldn't believe Ballard was right, because if my Tourette's wasn't what made me unlikable, something else did. My tics might slow with age, but what if they weren't my problem in the first place?

Unaware of my deep thoughts, Ballard went on in usual Ballard fashion. "Clara said her friend's having a party in Dadeville this weekend. I'm gonna drive over. I met this girl, Christie-Ann. She may be my prom date. Wanna go?"

There was no way Ballard could date the same girl from now until prom in April. No way in hell. The Crimson Tide falling to the University of Kentucky was a more likely occurrence than Ballard dating one girl, and one girl only, for more than about two weeks.

"Sorry, not this weekend."

"Why? What's going on this weekend?" Ballard swirled a French fry in a pool of watery ketchup.

"Nothing. I'm just burned out on parties." I watched his fry circle slowly.

"I don't get you, Stephen. I don't get you at all."

After school, I took my time gathering my books and leaving. I stopped by the counselor's office to drop off some papers from my last neurology appointment. They'd all go into my file alongside my 504 plan and a billion other reams of paper from all of my years in Moorhen and even some from before, records from Auburn that got transferred when we made the move.

Leaving, I had to go down a flight of stairs by the library. At the top of the steps, I paused to watch a couple walking below. They were arguing. When the girl turned, I caught sight of a blue streak in her hair. It was Joan.

Joan and Wade.

I leaned over the cement wall and watched them. They paused by the library doors. Joan wiped her eyes.

Wade's deep voice boomed out over the sidewalks, "Fuck you, Joan."

Her hands were in fists by her side, and I waited, expecting her to punch him like she had all those years before. *Go on. Break his perfect nose and take him down a notch or two.*

She didn't though . . . she didn't punch him or even slap him like some girl in a chick flick. She cried, wiping her eyes again.

"I'm so tired of you crying all the time," Wade said. "This is why we broke up in the first place."

Wade opened the door and went inside. I was shocked,

but not by the conversation. I couldn't believe Wade Bond was going into a library. No way did he read.

"Who knew she could cry?"

I turned to find Erin standing a few feet away, watching the same scene I was. "What?"

"Joan," Erin said. "She acts so tough all the time, walking around like she owns the place."

Erin was a little bit right. Sylvie was pretty much Joan's only friend. Most guys steered clear of her because of her dating Wade and all. Except, she wasn't dating Wade, not anymore. They'd broken up, but here she was, crying to him outside the library.

As I took a step, planning to go ask if she was okay, Joan opened the door and followed Wade inside.

However tough Joan wanted the world to believe she was, she looked like a kid who just dropped her ice cream cone.

Erin frowned. "She'd be better off without him."

"Yeah," I said.

There was an awkward pause. Erin and I were friends, but we didn't talk much at school, just at church, since we didn't have the same classes this year.

She adjusted her backpack straps. "Anyway, I came to find you because Matt wants me to ask you again about playing in the youth band. He said your mom said you were learning guitar."

"You know I'm not going to play in that band. Besides, I just started learning. I'm not good yet." My shoulder jerked, and Erin either didn't notice or pretended not to.

"I figured. I told him you'd never get on stage in front of the whole church."

"Thanks," I said.

She shrugged. "No problem. You know how Matt is when he gets an idea. If I can't convince you, he will have your mom start bugging you next."

"He means well," I said.

"Yeah, anyway, I'm running late for yearbook." Erin opened the door to go back inside. "You coming this way?"

"No, I'm headed home."

"See ya, Stephen." The door creaked closed behind her.

I took the steps slowly, hoping Joan would come back out. Maybe she went in and gave Wade a piece of her mind. Maybe I'd misread the entire situation.

She never reappeared though, and I unlocked Gwinn the Schwinn from the bike rack and pedaled toward home, my mind swimming with girls and all the ways I simply did not get them. I understood girls about as well as my father understood me.

That is to say . . . not at all.

There were people I didn't know at our house when I walked in after school.

I'd planned to get straight to my math homework. The sooner it was out of the way, the sooner I could relax. Two men were standing by my bedroom door, staring at the end of the hallway like any minute the wall would open up to reveal Jesus himself, seated at the right hand of God the Father coming again to judge the quick and the dead. I was tempted to repeat the Apostle's Creed or the Lord's Prayer or something, maybe take communion right there on the hardwood floor.

Or maybe I just spent too much time at church.

"Hi," I said instead.

Both men turned to look at me. One wore a John Deere cap and the other wasn't much older than me. He had on cargo pants and a Moorhen High T-shirt exactly like the one Ballard wore over the weekend, only this one was faded to a grayish color instead of the sharp navy of Ballard's.

I might've recognized him. Maybe he'd graduated the year before. I wasn't sure.

"Oh sorry, bud, guess I'm in your way." The older man moved to one side and let me in my bedroom door. I closed it behind me and listened through it as the men discussed the best strategy for knocking out the wall they were staring at.

I looked at the carpet, faded almost the same shade as the stranger's shirt, and watched my foot jerk. My body was heavy and slow. Around me, my room looked exactly as it always did, slightly messy but in a way that made sense to me. There was order, even if it wasn't an order my mother would ever comprehend.

My mind wasn't clear though. It was like I'd gone to that party and found a couple of strangers standing around inside me, debating the best way to proceed with what sounded like destruction. I was pretty sure the men in my hallway had a good reason for wanting to knock out a wall, but I wasn't so sure about the strangers in my mind.

Something had gotten knocked loose.

After the men outside my door left, I found Mom sitting on her bed with her ancient laptop.

"What's going on?" I asked.

"I'm making a Pinterest board." She clicked something on the screen.

"For what? And I was talking about the men in the hall. The ones planning to rip out a wall in our house." I sat on the foot of her bed. It was covered in a green and blue quilt my great-grandma made.

"Inspiration for the new office space, which is what those guys will be building." She looked up from her computer. "I've been saving for a while so I can build your dad a writing room, somewhere he can spread out. It's his Christmas present this year."

"He has a writing room." I pointed in the general direction of my father's computer room.

"Sweetie, that's a closet. Or a pantry, technically. It's supposed to hold canned goods. There are no outlets, and he can hear every sound the rest of us make."

And we can hear every sound he makes.

We lived in an old mill house, two bedrooms, one bathroom, and a two-car garage the last owners added on. She was right about the outlets. I tripped over bright orange extension cords at least twice a day. But my father never complained about the cramped space.

"Can't he use an office at The Exchange?" It was logical to me, and it would get him out of the house more often. I hardly ever got the whole place to myself the way Ballard got his house all summer while his parents worked and his siblings went to camp.

My parents are both active people. When we are all home, they want to talk and do household projects. I like my alone time though. I like time to process without needing to explain that processing to Mom and Dad.

Mom frowned. "There's no space at the church, and you know it. We're packed in as it is. Besides, while we're doing this, we'll also be adding a second bathroom. You won't have to share with Dad and me anymore."

Now that was the kind of building project I could get behind.

I wandered back into the hall, where the older man had returned and was making notes on a yellow legal pad. The younger guy had been replaced by a middle-aged man in overalls. Since the men were, once again, blocking my bedroom door, I decided it was a good time for a bike ride. Math homework could wait.

When I pedaled out of the garage, I almost rode right into one of the guys I'd seen inside.

"Whoops." I put on the brakes. "Sorry."

"No worries, man." He was leaning against our rolling green trash can, smoking a cigarette. His hair was long and blond, held back by a blue rubber band.

My shoulder jerked and I sighed. The boy didn't mention the tic, but I knew he noticed it. "I have Tourette's," I said. May as well get it out of the way. If these guys were going to rip out our hallway and add two rooms, odds are they'd be over at our house every day. We'd be seeing a lot of one another.

His eyes lit in recognition. "I remember. You sat at my lunch table at Moorhen, with your buddy Ballard, right?"

Yes! That's why I knew him. He was a senior when we

were freshmen. His girlfriend's best friend dated Ballard for a while, and we got to sit at their table. It didn't last long. It never does with Ballard, but I remembered the guy.

"Nick Dane," I said. "It's been a while. Sorry I couldn't place you earlier."

"No worries, man," he said again. "You're better though, right? You seem better."

"What do you mean?"

"I mean, your twitching or whatever was bad. Like, your legs used to bump up on the underside of the table and shake everything. We never said anything, 'cause, you know, it wasn't like you did it on purpose, man. But you're pretty still right now."

His voice had a low undulating rhythm. Like if a surfer dude moved to small town Alabama and smoked a few joints and listened to Bob Marley. It wasn't annoying, though. He was relaxed and my twitchy self envied him. A lot.

"I guess I'm better, most days. Freshman year sucked." I remembered my feet and knees hitting the undersides of tables and desks that year. I worried the bruises would never heal, the bruises on my knees and the mental bruises left by Wade and his friends.

"Always does, bro. Always does." He nodded sagely, like he'd said something deep.

I almost argued with him. I'm sure there are sucky things about freshman year for everyone, yeah, but I was convinced I had it worse.

Maybe every high school freshman is nervous and a little lost when they show up at their brand-new school, surrounded by older kids, but how many of those kids get dragged down the hall by a scarecrow-singing football player? How many of those kids fall down the stairs because their legs are jerking so bad on a regular basis? How many of those kids are forced to use the elevator to *avoid* falling down the stairs?

But I knew better than to argue with Nick. People who didn't live with Tourette's syndrome had no idea. To them, it was just some twitches. Or else it gave me carte blanche to yell out cuss words in the middle of class.

"So . . ." I could've ridden off, but Nick was a popular guy when he was at school. Chatting with him would give me something cool to tell Ballard about during lunch on Tuesday. "You work in construction now?"

"With my dad, yeah." He nodded toward the yellow truck parked on the street. The logo on the door was a giant dog in a spiked collar. It read "Great Dane Construction."

"Weren't you enlisting in the army?" I turned away from the truck and back to Nick.

"Air force," he said. "Messed that up, man. I messed that shit all kinds of up." He didn't sound angry or even frustrated. He could've been telling me he had turkey for lunch or my shoe was untied.

There was something else about Nick, something dancing at the corner of my brain, but I couldn't put my finger on it. One simple fact tiptoed past my periphery. I shook my head and twisted my hands on the handlebars.

Nick took a long drag on his cigarette, staring off into space, so I got a good look at his profile, the bump midway down his nose, and the watery blue of his eyes.

Then it hit me.

"Joan," I said, startling myself. I hadn't intended to say it out loud.

"Joan?" Nick tilted his head to the left and blew out a stream of smoke.

"You used to give Joan Pearson a ride to school sometimes."

I felt silly saying it, like I cared who gave Joan rides.

He nodded, his gaze settling on something in the distance.

"I gotta go." I steeled myself for one last leg kick and put my feet on the pedals.

"No worries, man." That appeared to be Nick's favorite phrase. He managed to use it three times in a three-minute conversation. "See ya around."

I told him goodbye and rode down my driveway, turned right by the mailbox, and headed for the Tallapoosa. I was sitting in a gazebo alongside Lost Bridge Trail when my phone buzzed.

Hey. It's Pilar. I'm texting so now you have my number.

I made myself pause, fingers over the keyboard. My heart thrummed with excited energy. I'm not sure what I was really feeling though. Happy, yeah. She was pretty and easy to talk to. And being easy to talk to *was* a big deal, despite what Ballard said at lunch.

But if she was texting me, she must not know about the rest of the party. It was possible she didn't know those girls at all. And with them kissing so many guys, I doubt they were passing my name around as some major conquest. No one would even pass my name around as a minor conquest. I liked Pilar. How I automatically smiled when I saw her text had to mean something, right?

Hey, I wrote back. *How are you?*

I know. Brilliant and interesting I was not. Text conversations were possibly harder than in-person conversations. The only good thing was no one could see my tics when we were texting.

Good. Procrastinating studying for a math test.

I'm procrastinating math homework too. Great minds think alike.

She didn't reply. I waited, dumbly staring at my phone screen for three or four minutes. Another cyclist rode by and a couple with a kid in a jogging stroller. They all waved. My tics were pretty controlled while riding, and anyway, people only saw each other in short flashes as they crossed paths. I recognized some faces of regular walkers and riders, but mostly I was anonymous here in the woods, a generic teen boy on a bike.

When it was clear Pilar wasn't going to text again, I slid the phone back into my pocket and left the gazebo. The sun would go down soon, and I did have math homework to get done.

I considered calling Pilar and telling her about the other girls I kissed the night we met, about the experiment and what a crappy person I was. But I didn't. I was too glad she didn't know. There was a good chance she'd never find out, right? We didn't know the same people, so there was no one to tell her.

Besides, it's not like we were dating. It was only a conversation at a party, one kiss, one night. It didn't mean anything serious was going on, but I was uneasy, like everything inside me was leaning just a little to the left.

I opened a new text to Pilar, but the phone rang.

"Hello," I said, putting on my talking-to-parents voice.

"Hey, bud, Mom wants us to go out for dinner. She's tired of the noise here. You close by?"

"Yeah, I'm just at Lost Bridge."

"Head on home, then. Be careful."

"On my way. See you at home."

I slid the phone back into my pocket and headed back into town.

I would text Pilar again soon, but first I would figure out what I actually wanted to say.

Chapter Seven

Sunday night, I rode my bike over to The Exchange, planning to slip in the back quietly and hope my parents didn't notice my late arrival. I would've been on time, but Ballard wouldn't shut up about another potential prom date, the percentage of single girls at local high schools, and the plan he had for convincing his fantasy prom date he was the perfect guy to be her first.

I had no input for him, and kept trying to change the subject. The way he talked about girls used to be amusing, but lately his heart didn't seem in it. Under his player attitude, cracks were forming. Mostly, despite all his talk, I hadn't seen him with an actual girl in a while. It had all become theoretical.

I arrived at church distracted by my own theoretical girl problem. Pilar hadn't texted again. I wasn't disappointed as much as confused. Our text exchange Monday was innocent enough, and I couldn't see any way my messages might've made her shut down the conversation.

Distracted, I locked my bike and let myself in the offices so I could use the mall entrance to the theater area. That route took me past the bathroom, where I stopped to wash my hands and run my fingers through my hair.

whatever brought these two prideful creatures to the point of public debacle.

"Joan," Mrs. Pearson said, all attempts at whispering given up as hopeless. "Your dad won't listen. I'm trying to survive this until he gets better."

"He's not getting better," Joan snapped. "He's only getting worse. Where the hell is he, Mom? Where did he drive off to this morning before the sun even came up?"

"He has a job interview. In Mississippi." The explanation sounded weak, Mrs. Pearson's voice devoid of the confidence it held in school hallways and assemblies. "His truck has been making funny noises. He can't afford to take it in right now, so he took the Suburban."

"I don't believe that, and neither do you. He's in no shape to go to a job interview."

"Fine. You do not have to believe me. You do not have to do this thing for me, this one thing. Go on and leave. Go on and do what you want to do. I know what you get up to with the boys and the drinking. I'm not stupid. I know things you do not know I know."

"No, Mother, I'll stay. God forbid I have any life of my own. Whatever. I'll wait for you. But I'm not going in there and listening to some crackpot preacher talk about a God who doesn't give a shit about me."

"Carrie Joan," her mother gasped.

There was silence in the lobby. I almost peeked around the wall, but Joan sighed. "I'm sorry, Mom. I know you need to believe God cares. But I don't."

Then came the sound of high heels clicking across the tile.

They moved in the direction of the theater. A door opened and loud music poured out. It got quiet again. I would've stayed hidden until Joan left, but she didn't leave. Instead, there was a thump and soft sobbing.

For the second time that week, I was witness to a crying Joan. Talk about topping the list of things I never expected to happen.

Ever.

I was torn. Obviously, it was none of my business, and I seriously doubted I was the best person to handle Joan's crisis of faith or lack of faith or whatever was going on there. My own religion was iffy. The God Joan's mother believed in, the God my mother preached . . . He was the same God who made me . . . the God who made me have Tourette's syndrome. Maybe there was some grand purpose, but most days it just sucked.

I did believe in God. Mostly because Jesus was a bit of a smart-ass, and he didn't give a shit what anyone thought about him. I was square with a guy like that, a guy who went around doing good things and pissing people off by not conforming to their stereotypes. I just wasn't so good at dealing with his daddy, if you know what I mean. God and me had some differences of opinion.

If you judge by the Garden of Gethsemane scene in the gospels, I'd say Jesus and his daddy had some differences of opinion themselves.

But there was a girl crying on the floor of the theater lobby, and eventually some church member would need to use the bathroom. They would find Joan crying. She was exposed, and I knew what it was like to be exposed. Plus, she'd saved my rear once before. Even if it backfired and I wished she'd kept her damn fist to herself all those years ago.

I stepped from behind the wall and my foot kicked out, followed by a triple shoulder jerk and a grimace. Talking to a sobbing Joan was terrifying, and my body told me so in every way it could. No way could she miss my entrance, what with all the fanfare of a circus ringmaster my tics orchestrated.

She raised her head. Her eyes were red-rimmed. Her cheeks were wet. They looked so soft, I thought about touching them with my fingertips.

"Stephen?" She wiped her eyes quickly.

"Hey, Joan. Sorry, I'm late for the service, and I heard you and your mom. I shouldn't have listened, but I did, and maybe you'd rather not be out here in the lobby when people come out. They'll dismiss all the teenagers for youth in a few minutes." All of those words tumbled out of my mouth in a heap, each one rushing to get out faster than the one before it.

"Oh." She glanced over her shoulder, toward the theater. "Right. I should go."

"If you want to wait on your mom somewhere private, I know a place." I could've let her leave. I could've watched her walk out the glass doors into the steamy August night.

There's this theory I heard once, about changing the past. Something about dropping a rock into a river so the current parts, but as the river flows on, the current comes back together. It corrects itself. So, no matter how hard you try, the inevitable remains the inevitable.

"Thanks," Joan said. "That'd be great. I'm a bit of a mess right now."

I nodded and steeled my shoulders against another jerk. "Follow me."

And she did. Joan hopped up off the tile floor and followed me down the hall, past the worship service in progress, to a locked door in a dimly lit corner.

"Where are we going?" Joan asked, leaning against the faded red wallpaper.

"You'll see." I pulled a key ring from my pocket and flipped keys until I found the one I wanted. The door opened with a low creak and I ushered Joan inside, where we were greeted by a narrow staircase. I used my phone as a flashlight to guide us up the steps.

"Can we turn on a light, maybe?" Joan whispered, sounding oddly reminiscent of her mother a few minutes earlier. I decided it was best not to point out any similarity between them.

"No," I said. "The projection room has windows into all of the theaters. If we turn on the overhead lights, the windows will brighten and everyone in the worship service will turn to look."

At the top of the stairs, there was a tiny lamp. I clicked it on only because it emitted about as much light as a birthday candle.

"That's something at least," Joan said.

"You can always go back to the lobby." I questioned my sanity for offering to help her in the first place.

"No, thanks. I'm not complaining. It's just . . . going into a small pitch-black room with a guy usually means something other than what I think this means."

"What do you think this means?" I shoved a pile of old cardboard boxes to one side and motioned for Joan to sit.

She chewed her lip a moment and studied my face. "I think it means you're being nice. But I'm not sure why."

"I'm a nice guy," I said, turning to go.

"Hey, wait, where're you going?" She toyed with an old projector wheel, empty of film, but her eyes were on me.

"To youth," I told her. "You didn't seem like you were in the mood for company."

She patted the thick carpet beside her. "Stay. Please? It's sort of creepy up here."

I was torn again. Saving Joan from public humiliation was one thing. Hanging out with her in the projection room was another. On the one hand, Matt would notice my absence when it came time to make espresso over in the youth room. I was his best barista, master at doodling hearts in cappuccino foam, though he preferred I doodle crosses. To me, it was a bit morbid to draw the death penalty in a cup of coffee.

On the other hand, I was curious about Joan's distress. Her mother had developed an attachment to my mother, which wasn't strange by itself. Lots of people turned to Mom when they needed help, but I'd never seen Mrs. Pearson as anything but a teacher, someone who already knew everything. The voice in the lobby earlier had been broken and a little desperate. And here was Joan, who once punched Wade Bond in the face for me and later made him her boyfriend . . . and she was a wreck.

"Come on, Stephen. There's something I've always wanted to ask you. Stay a minute?"

"Okay," I said. "For a bit."

Her hands dropped to her sides. "I am obviously in distress here. I'm sure there are mascara streaks across my face, and I'm huddled on the floor of a dusty room."

Her dark eyes shone with victory as I sat beside her on the floor, not sure if that was my choice or if I'd been expertly manipulated.

"What have you always wanted to ask me?"

She used the hem of her T-shirt to rub the mascara from her face. When she lifted it up, I couldn't help but peek at the strip of skin showing above her jeans. It was a warm brown color, her belly button like a tiny eye winking at me.

She lowered her shirt. "Back when we were in middle school, why did you hate me so much?"

I crossed my arms and leaned my back against the wall, not looking at Joan. "I never hated you."

"Yes, you did," she said. "I tried to be your friend, and you were mean. If I sat by you at lunch, you moved. If I spoke to you in the hall, you ignored me. I got your phone number from Ballard and you hung up on me."

She was right. I had done all of those things.

"So, tell me why."

When I didn't answer right away, she nudged my shoulder with hers.

I schooled my features, a grimace threatening, and sighed. "I can't believe you don't know."

Something buzzed. Joan's cell. It was in her pocket, and her hip was so close to mine the vibration hummed against me. She pulled out the phone and we both looked at the caller ID. It was my blond-haired nemesis in his football jersey. His name flashed cheerfully on the screen.

"Go on," I said, almost a challenge. "Answer it."

She shook her head and tapped ignore. The buzzing stopped. The screen went blank, and she slid the phone back into her pocket.

I wasn't sure what to make of her choosing to skip Wade's call and keep talking to me, but it was enough to convince me I may as well tell her the truth. "You punched Wade. In my defense, you punched Wade. You humiliated him."

I snuck a look at Joan. Her eyes were pure confusion. "You care about Wade?"

"I don't give a fuck about Wade," I snapped. Lowering my voice, I said, "But I do care about me. And when you pulled that stunt in the hall, I never heard the end of it. 'Stephen Luckie, lucky thing his girlfriend's around to protect him' and 'Lucky his bodyguard showed up.'"

She shifted on the carpet and met my eyes. "You were mad at me for sticking up for you? Wade was being a jerk. Someone had to do something."

I didn't understand how she could not understand. "No, someone didn't."

"Well, Stephen, *lucky* for you, I never did it again." Her mouth looked sort of like my grimace.

"Whatever." A tic was looming and, sure enough, my shoulder jerked three times.

"Does that hurt?" she asked, the anger draining from her voice.

I preferred anger to pity, so I wasn't thrilled with the change. "No. Does it hurt when you shrug?"

She shrugged her shoulders quickly and shook her head.

"It's the same muscles," I said. "Only I don't choose when they move."

"Are you ever still?" It was a genuine question. No one had asked me before. Unless you count an exasperated elementary school teacher throwing her hands up and saying, "*Don't you ever hold still?*"

"Sometimes," I said. I remembered kissing Sylvie and Pilar and the girls at the party. I didn't tell Joan about those times though. I picked something safer. "When I'm nervous and the tics get bad, Mom will reach over and put her hand on my arm or my leg. It can calm my muscles for a while."

Joan nodded. She slowly reached her right hand across the space between us and touched my jerky left shoulder. The angle forced her close to me, her body tilted forward.

I turned to look at her face, my shoulder alive with the heat of her warm fingers through my cotton shirt. That close, her eyes weren't black. They were coffee brown. She'd missed a smudge of mascara and I instinctively wiped it away with my thumb. Our faces were so close I spotted an eyelash fallen on her cheek.

I could kiss her. She'd let me.

"Stephen!" Mom's voice rang out at the bottom of the stairs. "Stephen, are you up there?"

For a split second, neither of us moved. Then, Joan took her hand from my shoulder and stood up. I stood up too.

"Yeah, Mom. I'll be right down."

"Matt needs your help," Mom said, her steps quick on the stairs. I tried to think fast, but my shoulder was already shrugging and my foot kicked out. Mom appeared in the doorway. "Oh. You must be Joan."

"Hi." Joan gave a halfhearted wave. "Sorry, Reverend Luckie. My mom and I had a fight and Stephen offered to let me chill up here until I calmed down."

I watched doubt flicker across Mom's face. It was a new situation, catching me alone with a girl.

"I'll go help Matt," I said and darted past Mom, leaving her and Joan to work things out. Joan wasn't my problem. Whatever seemed to be about to happen . . . I was imagining things. I blamed it on the experiment. With all that craziness, my brain must've decided every girl wanted to kiss me. They were all waiting to corner me in a dim projection room.

I was such an idiot, letting my guard down with Joan.

Not ten minutes after I started pulling espresso shots with Matt, we ran out of straws for the smoothies. I knew where the extra straws were stored, behind the old snack bar in the theater lobby. I crossed back through the offices and ducked behind the counter.

When I stood up, straws in hand, I caught sight of Joan. She was standing on the sidewalk outside the doors. The light of her phone screen illuminated her face. I wanted to apologize for running off like I had, leaving her with my mother. But as I approached the exit, a silver Lexus pulled to a stop at the curb. No one got out to open the door for her, so Joan did it herself and slid into the passenger seat. The windows were tinted, and the sun had long since gone down, so I couldn't see the driver. It didn't matter though. I knew the car.

While I stood in the bright lobby, holding straws and feeling like an idiot, Joan rode away with Wade, her knight in shining armor.

"Stephen?" Erin poked her head into the snack bar area and looked around until she spotted me.

"Yeah, sorry. I got the straws."

"Cool, but that's not why I was looking for you."

I walked back around the counter. "What's up?"

"A bunch of us are going to hang out at Matt and Kelly's after youth. You want to come?"

I paused, considered going home and sitting alone in my bedroom, doing homework to distract myself from my anger over Joan and Wade. "Okay, yeah, I'll come."

"Good. You haven't been around much lately. We miss you."

I wasn't so sure that was the truth. Erin might miss me, but I wasn't tight with anyone in The Exchange's youth group. Still, when Matt hosted hangout time at his house, it was always fun, whether we watched some old movie or played ridiculous board games.

I took Matt the straws and got back to work. Erin stayed nearby, sitting on the counter with her legs dangling. We were both quiet, and I should've paid attention. I should've at least talked to her, asked what was on her mind, but my own mind was too full of Joan.

When we left after church, Erin walked beside me, arm swinging close to mine. My dad was always on about being a gentleman so I made sure she got to her car safely.

Before opening the door, she paused, the parking lot lights illuminating her freckled shoulders. "Was that Joan Pearson you were talking to earlier?"

I blushed. Who knows why, nothing happened with Joan. "Yeah, she brought her mom to church."

"Oh, well, that's nice." Erin was acting weird. She chewed her bottom lip and dropped her keys.

I bent over to pick up the keys, and she knelt beside me.

"You like Joan, don't you?" she asked.

I froze. "What?"

"I mean, there's nothing wrong with that, if you do." She grabbed her keys and stood up. "It's just, she isn't exactly a Christian."

I stood up as well, my brain screaming warning signals. "Joan's just a friend, and I don't care if she's a Christian or not."

"Okay." Erin's cheeks were pink, but maybe that was just a trick of the light. She fiddled with her keys and then turned to unlock her car door. "See you at Matt's, right?"

"Actually," I said, bothered by her comment on Joan's religion, or lack thereof. "I don't think I'm going. I forgot some homework."

Erin could be pretty judgmental, and I'd had enough

drama for the night. I just wanted to go home, not stick around for a lecture on evangelism or whatever spiritual issue was eating at Erin.

"Oh. Well. See you at school, then." She closed her car door and started the engine.

I left for home, determined to steer clear of drama from now on. No more kissing experiment. No more eavesdropping on family fights. No more awkward time with Erin. It was time to focus on just one girl, and if she ever texted back, that girl would be Pilar.

Chapter Eight

Here's the thing about the moment that might've led to a kiss with Joan in the projector room: as much as I insisted to myself I'd imagined the whole thing, and as often as I remembered her riding away in Wade's car, my stupid heart was snagged on a smudge of black mascara and those damn deep brown eyes.

While I pulled a shot of espresso in the youth room, Joan made herself comfortable inside my brain, her hand moving toward my shoulder again and again. The kid would walk off with his overdone latte and I'd stand there, staring into space, until Matt nudged me to get back to work. The rest of August passed this way.

Mrs. Pearson kept attending The Exchange, but Joan didn't show again. I wasn't surprised. She didn't want to be there in the first place, and there was no reason for her to go back, no matter how hard I tried to come up with one.

I smiled at Mrs. Pearson when I passed her in the hall at church, but seeing her after hearing about Joan's dad made me thankful she wasn't my English teacher. It was awkward knowing personal things about your teachers. Not that I knew anything personal, just that there was something personal to know, something to do with Mr. Pearson. It was enough to make my eyes cling to Joan in a crowd at school, and to lead me in a new route to some of my classes, avoiding the hall where Mrs. Pearson stood outside her door, directing traffic.

The third week of September, with the tips of the leaves painted yellow and the demolition of our back wall beginning, I finally got a text message from Pilar.

I was riding my bike on Lost Bridge Trail, mentally analyzing the small amount of data from my short-lived kissing experiment. I was almost to the gazebo, exactly where I'd been the last time Pilar texted me. I could've taken it as some sort of confirmative sign, but I didn't usually see omens in random occurrences.

Anyway, thinking about that party led me to a party Ballard was throwing. It would be a couple of weeks before Halloween and would involve various levels of costuming. The girls would inevitably choose to be sexy-something. Sexy witch, sexy cat, or else they'd be their favorite movie character. Half of the guys would make sad attempts at being funny. Last year, Ballard pinned Smarties candies all over his jeans and went as a "Smartie-pants." The other half of the guys wouldn't bother.

I was in the other half. After years of attempting to be invisible, I didn't have an urge to dress up and draw attention to myself.

My phone buzzed and I pulled off the trail to check the message.

I'm so sorry, Stephen. Mom took my phone when she found out about me going to that party with Isabel.

For over a month? I asked.

My parents are intense. Please don't be mad.

I stared at the screen. On the one hand, there hadn't been much room in my brain for Pilar since the never-really-happened-but-felt-like-maybe-something thing with Joan in the projection room. But, on the other hand, I'd spent the last few weeks trying to get up the guts to talk to Joan, to ask if she was doing okay, since I'd witnessed that nasty scene with her mom.

Talking to Joan was impossible. For being his *ex*-girlfriend, she sure was with Wade a lot. She went to all the football parties, and Ballard told me about how drunk she got, how she practically attacked some freshman girl who spilled a drink in her lap. Joan's behavior was more and more erratic, including a three-day suspension over a fight in the cafeteria.

Since I was still not willing to return to Ballard's ridiculous kissing experiment, my choice was to keep obsessing over an out-of-reach girl or test the waters with Pilar. The decision seemed obvious.

It wasn't, though. It wasn't obvious at all, and that should've been my sign, flashing lights and screaming sirens.

Stephen? Are you mad?

I had no right to be mad. She wasn't required to communicate with me.

No, I answered. *I'm not mad.*

I want to see you again, the next message read.

I wanted to see her again too. Whatever was *not* going on with Joan aside, Pilar was easy to talk to, super hot, and she'd even remembered me from when we were kids. It was nice to be memorable, to matter.

Me too.

Isabel is going to the mall Saturday, to meet her boyfriend. I can go with her if I want, so long as all of my homework is done.

I can meet you there, probably. I'll ask to borrow the car.

I called Mom. As much as I love Gwinn the Schwinn, she and I would not make it to Eastdale Mall in Montgomery. Not if I wanted to be un-sweaty and not covered in road grime when I arrived.

"The mall?" Mom asked. Her tone was hesitant. To her credit, I wasn't the hang-out-at-the-mall type, and when I did go it was with Ballard, so he drove.

"I want to see the new Marvel movie." I didn't want to explain about Pilar and her cousin.

"By yourself?" Mom asked. In the background, I could hear her printer running, loud motor whirring away on flyers for The Exchange's annual Trunk or Treat event.

"Yeah, Ballard doesn't want to go, and I really want to see it."

"Maybe I can go with you."

"Mom," I said. "I'm not going to a movie with my mother on a Saturday when half of my school will be there. They will *see* me."

I was exaggerating. A lot of kids might be there. It was the nearest mall to Moorhen. But it wasn't likely anyone would notice me. Still, she bought it, and that's what mattered.

"You used to like mother-son date night." Her voice was pouty, almost drowned out by the ancient printer.

"Yeah, and I used to be twelve. Things change." There was a minor twist of guilt in my gut over lying.

I texted Pilar, *I got the car. What time do I meet you?*

At 2, in the food court.

Ok. See you Saturday.

She replied with a happy face and a heart emoji.

I smiled at my phone.

Saturday morning, while I sleepily spooned Cheerios into my mouth and wiped milk off my chin, Mom sat at the kitchen table and made a dozen lists on long narrow paper. I didn't pay close attention, but one list was a menu and one included a lot of names.

"I'm planning a cookout for some families from The Exchange," she told me, even though I hadn't asked.

"Cool." I took another bite of cereal and slurped the milk from my spoon.

"Don't do that," Mom said, glancing up from her vast array of papers.

I slurped again. She glared, and I smiled innocently.

"I want to form a new small group." Mom chewed the end of her pen. Gross. "I'll ask the Harpers and the Greggs. Maybe the Islingtons as well. I'm going to do the cookout here at the house and see how they all get along."

Great, she wanted to host people at our house while it was under construction. Sounds like a grand idea.

I was about to burst Mom's happy hospitable bubble when suddenly the cookout *did* sound like a grand idea. If we'd been inside a cartoon, a bright yellow lightbulb would've popped on over my head.

"You should invite Mrs. Pearson and her daughter," I

blurted so fast milk flew off my lips. White droplets dotted the table, and I blushed.

Mom raised an eyebrow. "Hmmm . . . You mean the daughter I caught you alone with in the projection room?"

My cheeks got darker. "It wasn't what it looked like. Joan is . . . We hardly even know each other. She was upset and wanted to get away from people."

"Uh-huh." Mom watched me with hawk eyes, and I noticed wrinkles between her brows.

"I'm being serious." I used a napkin to wipe milk spittle off the tabletop. "I overheard Joan and her mom arguing. I bet Mrs. Pearson could use some friends, like in this small group thing you're talking about."

Mom put her pen between her teeth and nodded. She always nods when she's deep in thought. Dad calls her Bobblehead Renee, as if my mother will become so famous one day, people will buy action figures of Reverend Renee Luckie, super pastor.

"Good call, Stephen." She scribbled "Yong Pearson" on the piece of paper. I'd never known Mrs. Pearson's first name.

My intentions weren't entirely pure though. Yes, Mrs. Pearson could benefit from a night out and Mom's new small group, but if she brought Joan, maybe I could finally get up the guts to talk to her. We wouldn't be around Wade or any of the popular football boys. We wouldn't be on her turf at all. Like in the projection room at The Exchange, we'd be on my turf—inside my comfort zone.

What I wanted to ask her in the projection room was about Wade, about how she could punch him in my defense and then make him her boyfriend. I had no reason to care. But I did. I cared.

I didn't need to leave for Montgomery until around one, but I had the car all day. I stood beside it with the keys and considered my options. In the end, I took Gwinn from the garage and rode to the river. I sat there a long time in the shadow of the bridge over the Tallapoosa, watching the water.

How would this date go with Pilar? Was it a date? I wanted it to be. I wanted to be doing a normal Saturday thing, like going on a cheesy mall date with a pretty girl, and Pilar was more than pretty. She was beautiful, with her river of hair and steel-spine confidence.

Joan was pretty in a different way. There wasn't a lot of softness to her, but those dark eyes pierced like needles with a good kind of pain—a know-that-you're-alive kind of pain. She was smart too, always on the honor roll list and taking AP classes. Joan was also unpredictable and sometimes downright mean.

Whatever reasons I had to care about her, she didn't give a rat's ass about me. We hadn't spoken two words since that night in the projection room. I shouldn't have suggested Mom invite her to the cookout.

I reminded myself she never went to church with her mother. She wasn't going to show up at my house for a barbecue.

By the time I started Mom's car and headed out of Moorhen, I'd promised myself to stop obsessing over Joan. It wasn't fair to go on a date with Pilar if my heart was stuck on someone else.

I didn't know what might happen with Pilar, but I couldn't find out without taking a few risks. Hanging out with her would be its own kind of experiment, way better than the kind Ballard had come up with, testing the waters of a possible future relationship.

Chapter Nine

The mall was crowded with families, and crowds make me nervous. Distracted by my pounding pulse, I tripped over a stroller on my way through the double doors. An angry toddler darted into my path not ten feet later. He reached his chocolate ice cream–covered hands out to keep from falling and smacked right into me.

I stumbled backward, felt my temper rumble in my gut, and took a deep breath. His mother scooped him up, apologized profusely, and disappeared back into the sea of people. My jeans were embellished by two brown handprints, but I was mostly still calm. Working with the preschool journey group at church taught me a lot of patience with kids.

I planned to duck into the bathroom and clean myself up, but as soon as I came into sight of the food court, Pilar spotted me.

"Stephen!" She waved excitedly and I waved back. The bathroom would have to wait.

Weaving between tables, she made her way to my side, grinning. She was just as gorgeous as I remembered. Her long hair was arranged in a complicated-looking braid to one side of her head. It hung over her shoulder and bounced when she walked. Once she was close enough, she threw her arms around me.

Surprised, I sort of stood there for a second before lifting my arms to return the hug. Without a moment's hesitation, she stretched on tiptoe and kissed me. Right there in front of all those people. A beautiful girl kissed me.

My whole body went still.

So much for taking things slow. Maybe I didn't have to say anything. Maybe I could hang out with her and see where it went. We were in public after all, not alone in a dark bedroom.

"Let's walk," she said when we broke apart.

I wanted to ask how we'd gone from texting a few times to strolling the mall holding hands and kissing where everyone could see, but I didn't. I mean, we kissed at the party, so kissing wasn't new, right? Her fingers were thin and slightly cold. I worried about my hand sweating as she swung our arms between us.

"What happened there?" Pilar examined the chocolate handprints on my jeans.

My shoulder jerked as I answered. "Some little kid branded me as soon as I got here. It's not going to come out."

"Maybe if we wash them right now." She tucked her bottom lip under her teeth.

"Right." I laughed. "How're we supposed to do that?"

"We need a sink. And a hand dryer. Come on." She tugged my arm so I'd follow her.

I expected her to send me into the men's room by myself to handle my stain situation in private. Instead, she took me to one of the department stores. As I trailed behind, people watched us, or watched her. A guy from school looked her over and waved at me. He was one of Wade's buddies. Football players didn't acknowledge my existence for any reason other than mocking me.

Inside the store, Pilar made turn after turn. She knew her way around the merchandise. A rack of half-price bathing suits, out of season, blocked her path, but she tugged me left, and we kept walking.

"Where are we going?" I asked.

"I told you, to wash your jeans. We need a bathroom."

She stopped, and I practically ran into her. We were standing in an alcove near the service desk, a phone ringing shrilly and a couple of salesgirls arguing about who was putting away returns. In front of us was a bathroom with a blue sign on the door and a little stick man in a wheelchair.

She opened the bathroom door and motioned me inside.

I stepped in.

And Pilar stepped in behind me.

I turned as she closed and locked the door, my heart speeding toward what her presence meant.

"You don't have to come with me." My voice cracked mid-sentence. I cleared my throat and tried again. "I mean, I'm going to rub a paper towel over the stain. It won't be entertaining."

"That's not good enough. Chocolate will set in fast. Trust me. I know about hand washing jeans. Our machine broke last month and I did my laundry and my little brother's in the bathtub for two weeks."

"Yeah, sure, but . . ." I looked at my pants and at Pilar, her hands planted firm on her hips.

"Are you being modest?" She dropped her hands and the defensive posture. "That's sweet, but don't worry about it. Boxers are exactly like shorts. It's not a big deal."

My face burned.

"What?" she asked.

I closed my eyes and didn't answer.

"Oh," she said, a tiny giggle escaping her throat. "You don't wear boxers, do you?"

"No." I sighed. "I don't like how they feel. Under my pants I mean. They get bunched up, and . . ."

Too much information, Stephen. Shut your mouth.

"Okay, no worries. Look, I won't tell anyone I saw you in your tighty-whities, okay?"

"It's not about people knowing you saw me in my tighty-whities," I told her, blushing furiously just saying "tighty-whities" to a girl. I didn't know how to explain the five billion insecurities warring for their chance to take me down a notch on what *should* be a fun afternoon at the mall with a pretty girl.

For starters, there would be no hiding the size and shape of things standing there in my briefs. I know a lot of guys measured against each other when they were kids, but I'd never done that. So I had no idea how I compared, or how many other boys she had seen nearly naked.

"Okay, how about this? If we both take off our pants, we'll be even. An 'I'll show you mine if you show me yours' kind of thing. Will that make you more comfortable?" She stood there, the bone of her hip peeking from the low rise of her jeans, threatening to undo every bit of willpower I possessed.

"No," I said. "It's fine. Please keep your pants on."

Pilar burst into a wild sort of laughter, tossing her head, so her thick braid swung.

"What is so damn funny?" I asked, not sure if I was being mocked. Usually when people laughed, it wasn't with me, but at me. I was shrugging my shoulder hard and ready to make a run for it.

"It's just . . ." She paused to catch her breath. "No boy has ever asked me to keep my pants on."

The part of me that reacted to being cornered responded before rational decision-making took over. "Do you take your pants off for a lot of boys?"

It was the wrong question. The laughter rushed from her face, instantly replaced by hurt and anger.

"I'm sorry." I groaned. "I didn't mean that how it sounded. I wasn't calling you—"

"A slut?" She arched an eyebrow while rebuttoning her pants.

"I didn't mean—"

"Forget it." She shook her head at me. "I did make it sound that way. So, to answer your question, no, not a lot of boys. Just two. Your turn. How many girls have you been with?"

My mind flashed on the girls I kissed after Pilar left the party. But still I didn't tell her about them. We were talking about activities that involved the removal of pants, and my stupid kissing experiment didn't count.

"None." I hated saying the word. It's not like I wanted to be some kind of man-whore and tell her I'd had sex with every girl at Moorhen. But admitting I was a virgin to a girl who wasn't . . . Well, it's not the way I wanted to spend a date, if a date was what it was.

"Okay. I get it. No girl has ever seen you without pants, and you're worried I'm going to be sizing you up or something, right?"

I nodded.

"Well, I won't be. I've had sex exactly one time with exactly one boy. It was dark and cramped, and I didn't see anything, so I have no previous sightings to compare with this one."

And that's how I ended up half naked, sitting on a toilet, while a gorgeous girl scrubbed chocolate off my pants in a department store bathroom.

I was skinny and exposed, my white knees almost as shiny as the porcelain sink. At least there was no need to talk. First there was the sound of running water and then the hand dryer blazing heat into my jeans.

Pilar handed over my pants.

She turned her back while I put them on. I tried to go fast, shooting my legs through the holes like bullets, but that led to me almost falling on my ass. Finally, zipper zipped, button buttoned, and belt buckled, I was clean and dry—chocolate free.

"Thanks," I said.

Pilar turned to face me, examining her work. "You're welcome. Can you believe no one tried to come in? I figured we'd get interrupted at least once."

I couldn't imagine explaining the situation. "Can you see us getting kicked out and me with no pants on?"

Pilar giggled and took a step toward the door, so we were standing very close. "You're cute, Stephen."

"I am?"

"Yeah, not like the guys I usually go out with. We are all alone in a locked room and you haven't even kissed me."

"It's not 'cause I don't want to," I said. "I don't have a lot of experience with this stuff."

I should've told her the truth, that I didn't know if I wanted her because of the obvious reasons . . . She was fun to talk to and every inch of her body made me tingle all over. Because that was enough. Before. But the thing with the kissing experiment happened, and I didn't like how I felt anymore.

I hated to admit my mom could be right. She was always talking about the importance of emotional connections before physical intimacy. It's as close as she came to giving me the sex talk, leaving the nuts and bolts of it to Dad.

"That's why I like you so much," Pilar said. "My last couple of boyfriends cheated on me, and it sucked, but if you aren't making a move when I am practically throwing myself at you, I'm guessing it's a safe bet you don't have three other girls hidden in your back pocket."

She had to use that number. Three. Exactly the number of girls I made out with right after her, exactly the number of girls I kissed without even asking their names.

The butterflies in my stomach turned to dragonflies. I don't remember what I said, if I said anything. I mumbled, not sure what to admit to and what to keep hidden. It's not like I was ever going to see those girls again. It's not like I had feelings for them.

And there wasn't anyone else either. Joan remained an odd fascination I couldn't shake, but not a relationship in any sense of the word.

Pilar hooked a finger through my belt loop and tugged me across the tile. My foot threatened a kick, but I pressed it hard into the floor and focused on Pilar's face, the way her lips parted.

Her fingers left my waistband, still warm from holding my pants under the dryer, and slid under my shirt, over my stomach. She went on tiptoe, and so what if I did kiss her? It was a tame kind of kiss, not like I'd let her take off her pants earlier. If Ballard changed places with me, he'd have had her naked so fast her head would've spun.

I kissed her, and I relaxed. All of the tension in my muscles disappeared, and when she nudged me backward, I bumped into the wall and pulled her closer.

Pilar ran her fingers through my hair and I kissed her neck, her collarbone. Her skin was warm and dewy. It was hot in the bathroom. When our mouths met again, I couldn't resist testing my limits. I fluttered my fingers near her breasts, nervous, and she whispered, "You can touch me, Stephen," in between kisses.

I wasn't sure how to touch her, though. I wanted to squeeze, but maybe that was wrong. I paused, like she might tell me what to do next, but someone banged on the bathroom door and we froze.

"Open up," a deep voice said.

Pilar giggled, and my shoulder jerked.

Busted, she grabbed her purse from the hook before opening the door. As we walked out past the security guard,

I'm sure my face was as red as his official mall staff polo shirt. Pilar, still giggling, ducked her head and moved quickly with me trailing behind.

"That was fun," Pilar said when we were out of the store, back in the sea of people and their loud voices.

Was it? I wasn't sure. It felt good. Damn good. But the day hadn't gone at all like I'd planned, and something Pilar said before we kissed suddenly exploded inside my head.

"My last couple of boyfriends cheated on me . . ."

If her last two boyfriends cheated on her, and she was saying I wouldn't cheat on her, did that mean I was her boyfriend? Had I become someone's boyfriend without even knowing if I *wanted* to be her boyfriend?

If Pilar noticed my confusion, she didn't comment on it, and I might've forgotten the whole thing. Might have. But I didn't.

We held hands and wandered in and out of stores. I bought us each an ice cream cone, and she sat on my lap while we ate. My leg twitched a couple of times, but Pilar didn't comment, and I enjoyed the looks we got. For the first time in my life, I wasn't invisible in a good way. Instead of people staring and wondering what was wrong with me, guys were staring like they wanted to be me.

I tugged Pilar's braid affectionately and she laughed. I liked making her laugh. And if I liked making her laugh, and I liked kissing her, and I liked being seen with her at the mall, maybe that was enough. Maybe that was my answer.

But I turned my head away from Pilar and looked across the food court. I don't know how my eyes found her in the crowd of people, like something about her called to me, my years-long fascination with Joan Pearson making me ever alert to the possibility of her presence. She was sitting at a round table, across from some of Wade's friends and another couple of girls. Her hair glistened under the fluorescent lights, and I couldn't make myself look away.

Joan turned and, at first, she seemed to look back at me, but Wade appeared, and she jumped from the table to greet him. When Joan moved, all of her moved. Her hips swayed, the yellow ruffles of her skirt swung, and her hair fell around her shoulders. Her arms settled beside her gracefully, like a dancer's, as she waited for Wade to walk into them.

He didn't.

Pilar followed my gaze. "Do you know her?"

"Who?" I asked, stupidly.

"The girl you are staring at so hard? Duh." She looked hurt.

"Yeah," I said. "From school. That's her boyfriend, Wade." As I said it, Wade sat at the table. He didn't hug her or kiss her or anything, and she deflated, dropping onto the bench beside him. It wouldn't help to explain Wade was her ex and not her current boyfriend. They were together so much, I'm not sure it mattered anyhow.

Pilar was watching me watch another girl, which was rude, no matter how unsure of everything I was. I didn't know how to save the situation, so I said the first thing that came to mind. "Wade's an asshole and she's a bitch."

It was a mean thing to say, mean in a way I don't want to be.

But in that moment, watching them together, I almost meant it. Part of me meant it. Part of me could not forgive Joan for loving a creep like Wade. Part of me was glad he'd snubbed her open arms in front of his friends and hers.

But another part of me?

A part I wasn't willing to acknowledge on that bench in Eastdale Mall . . .

That part of me leaned forward and kissed Pilar on her ice cream lips, tasting a girl who wanted only me, while pretending she was the girl that barely knew I existed.

"Your boyfriends were idiots," I told Pilar. "How could anyone cheat on you?"

She grinned and kissed me and then laid her head on my shoulder. "It's a good thing my taste in boys has improved. Maybe this new one won't be an idiot."

"He won't be," I said.

Why the hell did I say any of that? Simple, because I knew I was an ass for looking at Joan and wanted to make it up to Pilar. I know I was being confusing, but I was so damn confused myself, I let my mouth lead the way without any time for my brain to catch up.

I wanted to say something, anything, who knows what, but Isabel and her boyfriend appeared then. She was carrying a jewelry store bag, and he was holding her hand, glaring at Pilar and me on our bench.

"Pilar, kiss your boyfriend goodbye. Bobby has to work tonight." Isabel twirled the tiny shopping bag around her finger, a teasing smile on her lips.

Pilar didn't correct Isabel, didn't explain I wasn't her

boyfriend. She kissed me quickly and waved as they walked away.

Of course, I didn't correct Isabel either. I just sat there with my head full of static, happy and frustrated at the same time.

Chapter Ten

On Monday, I sought advice from the one person who knew how it felt to like a girl, even kiss a girl, and not be in a romantic relationship with said girl.

Ballard sat across the lunch table from me, spoon paused in midair. I'd explained my concerns, and he got an intense look on his face, as though I'd asked him to come up with a peace treaty for World War III or end the fighting between Israel and Palestine. Underneath his wild facade, Ballard could be serious. He liked to analyze things, which is why he came up with the whole kissing experiment in the first place.

"Did you ever say the word 'girlfriend'?"

I mentally inspected my Saturday at the mall with Pilar, the awkwardness with my pants and making out in the bathroom, and finally eating ice cream together until Isabel showed up and pried Pilar away.

"No," I told him once I'd replayed every bit of conversation from the day. "I never said the word 'girlfriend.'"

"Okay. Good." Ballard's spoon resumed its journey to the pudding cup in front of him.

Around us, the other guys rehashed a football game, and Sylvie sat cross-legged at the center of us all. She was wearing red leggings and a huge green T-shirt, making her look a bit like a Christmas elf who showed up too early. The bells jingling on her earrings helped the effect. Only Sylvie could pull off that outfit in September.

"But she said the word 'boyfriend.' Or, boyfriends, actually. And I didn't say anything to dissuade her."

"That is problematic," Ballard said. He licked his spoon and watched Sylvie eat a bite of salad.

"Right?" I folded and unfolded a paper napkin on the table. "I messed up, didn't I?"

"I'm not sure it matters," Ballard said. "I mean, if you don't want a girlfriend, tell her so. I know you think I string girls along too much, but I always tell a girl exactly where we stand. Otherwise, it gets messy fast."

He was right, and I knew it. But . . .

"What if I tell her I don't want a girlfriend right now, and she thinks that means I don't like her?"

Ballard shrugged. "Tell her it doesn't mean that."

"That seems too simple."

"Maybe it is. But you can't control how she responds, only how you act."

For a few minutes, we chewed in silence, the sound of the conversations around us rising and falling, Ballard's eyes continuously wandering to where Sylvie sat.

Then his eyes were back on me, and he looked like a cartoon lightbulb had just gone off inside his head. "We still have the kissing experiment, and you can't go around kissing other girls if you have a girlfriend."

"I'm done with that experiment, man. I have enough data to know it works, at least temporarily, but I'm not even sure it matters." I lowered my voice and leaned toward him. "Pilar likes me, right? And I didn't have to hide my Tourette's for her to kiss me."

"What are you boys discussing so intently?" Sylvie dropped onto the orange plastic seat beside Ballard.

"Whether or not Stephen here has a girlfriend." Ballard gave Sylvie an appreciative once-over. There was a certain glint in his eye that screamed trouble. His last prom date possibility turned out to be a hardcore virgin, wearing a silver purity ring and denouncing prom when he slipped it into conversation.

Sometimes I wasn't sure how Ballard and I stayed friends all these years. His perseverance in the prom quest and my discomfort with continuing the kissing experiment served to show how different my best friend and I had become, no longer riding bikes together or staying up all night with Legos and video games.

Well, okay, we still stayed up all night with video games. We'd just turned to *Call of Duty* instead of *Mario Kart*.

"How is that even debatable?" Sylvie wrinkled her brow. "Either you have a girlfriend or you don't have a girlfriend. It's not a sort-of-kind-of-maybe thing."

I blushed and suppressed a shoulder jerk. I held it off a total of three seconds. "I spent a day with this girl, and I'm afraid she thinks I'm her boyfriend."

"And you don't want to be her boyfriend?" Sylvie leaned against the table, the wide neck of her T-shirt gaping.

"I don't know," I said. "I like her. I might want to be her boyfriend . . . eventually."

"You're a good guy, Stephen. Most of these jerks wouldn't

worry about something like this." Sylvie cut her eyes at Ballard, who looked away innocently. "Tell me why you think she thinks you're her boyfriend. Did she say something about it? Call you her boyfriend to someone else?"

"She didn't call me her boyfriend, but she said her last boyfriend cheated on her, and she knows I won't do that. And I said they were idiots and implied I wouldn't cheat on her, but how could I cheat on her if she isn't even my girlfriend? So she must think she's my girlfriend, right?"

Sylvie ran a fingernail across her bottom lip. "Sounds like she was feeling you out, seeing if you were interested in taking the job of boyfriend. How many times have you seen this girl? Who is she? And why don't you ask her what she's thinking?"

"Her name is Pilar," I said. "We met at a party last month, and I've only seen her once since. I was going to talk to her Saturday, but she sort of . . . well, she took charge of things and I never found a good time to bring it up."

"Do you talk a lot? Like, on the phone or text or whatever?"

While I talked the situation over with Sylvie, Ballard had finished his pudding cup. He was sucking on the spoon and watching Sylvie intently.

I'd seen his look a million times before. It was always directed at something Ballard wanted but knew he couldn't have . . . a motorcycle most recently and, when we were kids, it was a friend's bike or video game or piece of candy. Usually, he got whatever it was he wanted.

But Sylvie? No way would Ballard get Sylvie. Rumor had it she was dating a college guy, some artist she met volunteering at the Shakespeare Festival. He went to Huntingdon College and had his lip pierced. Those are the facts I'd picked up from kids at church the week before.

"Okay, here's the deal. First of all, the talk has got to happen soon," Sylvie said.

"The talk?" My mouth puckered around the words, and I fought to straighten my lips out. "What talk?"

"The talk," she repeated, making air quotes so the glitter polish on her nails caught the fluorescent lights. "The 'what are we' talk. Figure out what you want and tell this girl. She'll appreciate your honesty. Girls like it when boys know their own feelings and aren't afraid to share them."

I nodded, processing the idea of a conversation with Pilar. I wasn't sure when I would even see her again, and "the talk" didn't sound like the kind of conversation you have over the phone. Maybe I could borrow the car again. She didn't live too far away. I could go see her after school one day, or over the weekend.

"But, for the immediate right now, no, you aren't her boyfriend. Either she wants you to be or she's seriously on the rebound and hoped you'd have sex with her."

I shook my head, fire in my cheeks. "No, Pilar isn't that kind of girl."

Sylvie shrugged. "I don't know if it's a certain kind of girl who has rebound sex, Stephen. All of us do things like that from time to time."

When Sylvie walked away, I felt a lot better. I hadn't accidentally landed myself in a committed relationship with a girl I barely knew, and I'd gotten through a whole conversation with Sylvie with only three or four tics, total. The more I talked to girls, the easier it got.

"I need a plan," Ballard told me, tapping his plastic spoon on the table. His eyes followed Sylvie, who tapped Joan on the shoulder a few tables away.

Joan was arguing with Wade, tears on her cheeks, and I looked away, embarrassed for her. A tough girl like Joan wouldn't want anyone to see her cry, but I kept managing to do just that. I couldn't figure out why she held on to Wade so tightly.

He was clearly moving on, Neva Calhoun sitting on one side of him with a leg thrown over his lap so her skirt rode up her thighs. I'd seen them in the hall together the week before, Wade's tongue so far down Neva's throat, you'd expect to see it sticking out of the girl's spinal column. While Joan left the cafeteria with Sylvie, Wade was sliding his hand up and down Neva's bare leg.

"You're not listening to me." Ballard chucked his spoon at my head.

"Ouch." I scooped the spoon off the ground and tossed it back at him, hoping he hadn't taken notice of who I'd been watching. "What do you need a plan for?"

"I need a plan to get Sylvie to go to prom with me."

I laughed. "Ain't gonna happen, man."

His face darkened. "Why the hell not? She made out with you, didn't she?"

The other guys at our table were gathering books and walking toward the exits. I wadded a napkin and shoved it into my brown paper lunch sack. "She kissed me because it was part of a game. She never would've done it otherwise. Besides, she has a boyfriend."

He rolled his eyes. "Some idiot with no money and no car. I can knock him out of play if I have a good enough strategy."

I didn't for a minute believe Ballard could convince Sylvie to go to prom with him, but I didn't say so again. After all, a few weeks earlier, I didn't believe any girl would ever want to kiss me, and there I was at lunch, having a conversation about my potential girlfriend and still feeling like shit for kissing girls I didn't even know.

"By the way," Ballard said when we were almost to our next class. "Party at Beckley Field Friday night. You should come. Bring Pilar."

I doubted I'd go to the party. I knew the kinds of things that happened there, and it wasn't my scene. Besides, Mom had that cookout planned for Saturday. I'd need to help her get ready for it.

As Ballard and I walked through the hall, my head was less static-filled. I had all week to figure out what I really wanted with Pilar. Since my nervous system has a mind of its own, it can be damn difficult to know how I feel.

After a week of daily text conversations with Pilar, I still had no idea if I wanted to be her boyfriend. I wanted to call her, but she said her parents would hear and know she was talking to a boy. They took her phone from her before dropping her off at school, and she only got it back when her homework was complete each day. I'd never known a kid my age with such strict parents.

My older sister dropped out, Pilar texted when I pointed out the ridiculousness. Part of me even suspected she was lying. She could have a boyfriend in Dadeville she didn't want me to find out about. Not that it mattered to me if she saw another guy at school. I wasn't her boyfriend, right?

I have to live in a cage to ensure my parents don't end up with two failures for daughters. My sister got her GED and pays her own bills, but they have these really traditional ideas about girls. We have to be perfect, beautiful, smart, successful. We have to be everything to be worth anything. It is so cliché, but my little brother, Matias, gets away with murder just for being a boy.

I wasn't used to the kind of long, chatty text messages Pilar liked to send. Ballard and I texted on occasion, answers to homework questions, cheats for video games, news about some girl he met at a game or party . . . Never more than a few words at a time. Mom and Dad sent me instructions, and sometimes Erin sent silly internet memes to make me laugh.

I didn't have any practice with the kind of conversations Pilar wanted in any scenario, but especially when typing on a phone screen, so I booted up my MacBook and opened iMessage. At least it let me type with all ten fingers. I hated typing in general. Flexing fingers could lead to awkward typos.

By Friday night, I was out of things to talk about, and pretty sure my Pilar attraction was entirely physical. So when Ballard texted he was picking me up for that party in the field I didn't protest. Joan might be there, and I was curious if the crying at school meant she and Wade were seriously over this time.

Mom was cleaning every inch of our house, because she'd decided to do the cookout as a lunch thing the next day instead of waiting till evening. It was getting dark too early already, and she wanted her guests to enjoy the beautiful weather.

"Also, it's supposed to rain around seven," Dad pointed out helpfully. He fiddled with the hallway plug. "The construction guys did something to the electricity. My charger keeps shorting out."

"Call them," Mom said. She poked Dad with the end of the broomstick on her way down the hall.

"It's too late," Dad said.

"Better call them late on a Friday than have our house burn because you didn't want to disturb them."

"I'm going to Ballard's," I called after her.

"Y'all have fun," Mom called back.

"Don't do anything I wouldn't do," Dad said as I slipped out the front door.

Things my dad wouldn't do . . . It struck me I had no idea what those things might be or what my father was like in high school. I doubted he was a Ballard, but I couldn't imagine he was a Stephen either. And definitely, *definitely*, Richard Luckie had never ever ever been a Wade.

I jogged down the front walk and slid into the passenger seat.

"Did you invite Pilar?"

"No. She's making me a little crazy," I said. "She texts all evening, from the moment she gets her phone back until she falls asleep, telling me everything I don't even want to know, like her best friend's favorite food and how many times she's already taken the ACTs."

"Oohh. Sounds serious, Stevie."

"Don't call me Stevie." I cringed.

Ballard laughed and drove off, blabbering on about girls wanting to keep us in prisons. He sounded a lot like Pilar talking about her parents, honestly, and I wanted to disagree with him. He seemed like such a jerk for bouncing from one girl to another so easily, but that night my perception shifted.

Pilar *was* crowding me, or thoughts of her were, even with a solid hour of driving between us. My tics had been fine on Monday, but as the week went on and her texts increased in length, my foot added a stomp to its typical kick out, and I sniffed badly enough Mom bought allergy meds just in case. Stressing over Pilar had wrecked my nerves, and I wanted to disappear into the woods and not worry about her intense feelings or the huge English project our teacher announced Thursday morning. I desperately wanted to get out of my head for a few hours.

Way out on the edge of town, backed up to the riverbank, was Beckley Field. We called it that because the Beckley family lived in an old farmhouse on the property. Josh Beckley, Ballard's cousin, hosted these huge parties in a clearing by the river. You had to park at the house and hike about two miles through the woods to get there, but it was worth it for the view.

Only now we were in high school, and it was all about beer and couples having sex behind oak trees. When we were in middle school we'd camp out—Ballard, Josh, and me—and I remember how clear and bright the stars were. I could use a big wide sky and no cell phone signal for a little while.

Even as I was thinking that, my phone buzzed in my lap.

Hey, my parents are out tonight. You can call.

I'm on my way to a party, I replied. *I won't have signal, but I'll call if I get home early enough.*

There was no reply, and when we crossed the city limit I pocketed my phone and let my mind wander away from Pilar. Ballard turned the music up, the amp he'd recently installed making the whole Jeep shake. As the bass thumped through my body, I decided I would get out of my own head that night.

I was on my way to a party, and I could figure out stuff with Pilar later. I'd heard Wade telling someone at school he was visiting his grandparents for the weekend, so the coast was clear as far as he was concerned. I could relax and not worry about being the target of some joke or another.

"This is going to be a good night," I said to Ballard.

He grinned. "The best night."

Chapter Eleven

The yard was packed with cars, and I spotted Josh's parents sitting on the front porch. His mom held a wineglass and his dad was nursing a beer. Speakers played Jimmy Buffett, and I was awed by the difference between these parents and my own. Mine would never buy alcohol for me, let alone half my school.

"Are we sure they're real parents and not alien-controlled parental bodies?" I asked as we walked past the front steps and around the house.

Ballard wrinkled his brow. "Sometimes I swear you're speaking another language."

Once in the woods, we met up with a couple more guys making their way to the party. Jimmy Buffett faded behind us, replaced by a country song I didn't recognize. Some people complained about the music at Josh's parties, but in the end, we live in Alabama. Country music rules the roost.

"How does he even get music out here?" one of the other kids asked.

While Ballard explained the logistics of speakers and sound, I tried to mask my sniffle by humming along to the tune. Eventually, we reached the field and I lost Ballard in the crowd.

I stood there like an idiot for a while, but I remembered Josh's old tree house and made my way around the edge of the field until I got to the river. There was a huge oak near the bank, and boards nailed to its trunk formed a ladder.

"Stephen?"

I turned to find Joan, her face scrunched as she checked to make sure it was me.

"I've never seen you at one of Josh's parties." She wore a green miniskirt and ripped tights.

"I don't usually come," I said. "To these parties, I mean. They're not my thing."

"But you're here now," she pointed out.

"I needed to get out of my house." My foot kicked and then came the stomp.

"I bet," Joan said, ignoring my foot. "Living with a preacher and all."

My stomach tightened. I hated it when people assumed things about my family based on Mom being a pastor. "Mom's not the problem. Mom is fine, good, perfect."

Joan frowned. "Okay, whatever. What's the problem?"

"Nothing." I didn't want to discuss Pilar with Joan.

"Fine, forget I asked. I was trying to be nice."

As she walked away Ballard called my name and waved for me to join him. A bunch of guys were passing around a bottle of Jack Daniels, and Ballard was grinning like an idiot and telling loud stories about two girls he met over the summer.

"What about it, Luckie?" Josh Beckley asked from his seat on a big rock beside Ballard. "You and Ballard are always together, right? Is he shitting us?"

I laughed nervously, willing my leg to remain stationary while I was standing so close to another person. A tic right then would've resulted in me kicking some kid in the thigh. I hadn't heard the start of the conversation, so I didn't know what they were talking about, but this was Ballard, so . . . "He's telling the truth. Well, he's telling the truth ten or fifteen percent of the time."

The guys all guffawed and one offered me the bottle. I shook my head and watched someone else pass it around.

"Yer jess jealous, Stephen." Ballard was drunk again. It was happening more often. He believed being drunk helped his life-of-the-party image. It didn't usually bother me, because I knew what it was like to desperately want acceptance.

"I'm not jealous, Ballard." I leaned against a tree trunk and sniffled.

He cocked his head to the side and smirked at me. "Nah, I guess you don't gotta be jealous, not with all the action you're getting lately."

There was a chorus of oohhs and some of the guys wanted to know what action I'd gotten, but I wasn't talking.

"He's got some chick from Dadeville jumping his bones in bathroom stalls," Ballard said.

"Shut up, Ballard." I clenched my fists tight in my pockets.

Ballard waggled his eyebrows and grinned bigger.

Around me, boys howled excitedly and slapped me on the back while I protested that it wasn't like that and glared hard at my best friend.

"Nah, nah, he's right, guys. It's not like that."

I was relieved. Ballard was going to take it back, smooth

it over. Instead, he launched into a detailed description of our "experiment," explaining how kissing was a magic treatment for Tourette's syndrome. After, instead of slapping me on the back in congratulations, the guys all gave me funny looks.

Rage boiled in my toes. It always started in my toes and leveled up second by second. I knew if I didn't get out of there fast, my head would swim and my vision would blur, and there was no telling what I would do.

I remembered a heavy bowl of punch, streamers and balloons, the sound of glass shattering and my mother sobbing.

I hadn't lost it like that in a long time, and I wasn't about to freak the fuck out in the middle of a party. If I was lucky, all of these guys were too drunk to remember what Ballard told them, but if I lost my shit and beat Ballard to a pulp, they *would* remember it.

"That's some kind of science test, the Scientific Method of Getting Lucky, right?" Josh snorted at his own joke, shoving his shoulder into mine. "Can I be your lab partner?"

I ran.

What the hell. I already looked like a complete idiot. Running off couldn't make me look much dumber.

I used to run in elementary school. Kindergarten was the worst. The tics hadn't started, but the big emotions had. My nerves were rubbed raw before I even left the house, and something always set me off in class. If we were on the playground, I'd run for the wooden equipment in the corner and hide behind it. If we were inside, I dived under the nearest desk and covered my ears. If there was something in my hand to throw, I threw it. If there wasn't, I'd sometimes grab a pencil or a stapler or whatever was handy at the moment.

That night in Beckley Field, I aimed my body at the big tree I'd left earlier and slammed hard against its trunk. The anger rising to my belly, making me sick, I pulled myself up the ladder and flopped onto the tree house floor.

Someone else was already there.

"Stephen?" The girl aimed her phone's light at my face.

No effing way.

I punched the wall, electric rage in my arms and fists.

No effing way.

Erin Mielke sat across from me.

"What are you doing here?" I asked.

"What are *you* doing here?" she shot back.

"Being pissed off." My leg jerked and I turned it into a kick, my foot thudding against the wall.

"Here." She held out a bottle of beer. There were a few more bottles lined up beside her.

I took the beer. "Thanks."

She was the only girl I didn't usually get nervous around, partly because she wasn't just a girl. She was pretty, with sandy blond hair and brown eyes. She had freckles and glasses with trendy dark frames that made her look a bit like Velma from *Scooby-Doo*. In a good way. But she'd been my friend since before I cared about girls in that way. She was just Erin. My friend.

"To answer your question, I came with Miles and he broke up with me about thirty minutes ago, in this tree house. But at least he left the beer." Erin raised her bottle in a mock toast.

I raised my bottle as well. "I came with Ballard and he made a fool out of me in front of everyone, so I came up here to keep from pulverizing his drunk ass."

We clinked the bottles and turned them up.

I don't love the taste of beer, and I don't normally drink, because my meds mean I get drunk faster than others. It's also just a bad decision to mix certain drugs with alcohol, but I was getting good at making bad decisions.

I vibrated with rage and hoped to God a sip or two would cool my nerves. I wasn't worried about Erin tattling on me. Despite our meeting with me under her desk in first grade, she'd always been pretty cool about things. Besides, if she told my mom, I could always tell her dad. We pretty much had to keep each other's secrets.

Not that we'd known each other's secrets for a while. Erin didn't hang around the same crowd Ballard did, and I only hung around Ballard. She was smart, but also a little weird. Her friends read big books and drove to Auburn to see plays at the Shakespeare Festival and hang out in museum cafés. I was a little surprised to find her nursing a beer at a high school party. She always seemed more mature than the rest of us.

"You always date college guys," I blurted after finishing the first beer and opening another.

"Not always." She shrugged. "Miles seemed different. He isn't though."

We sat in the quiet, and I watched stars through the skylight. Josh's parents went all out on the tree house when he was a kid. It had electricity too, or used to, but I didn't flip the switch to see if the lamps still worked. There was no reason to draw attention to ourselves.

"How'd Ballard make a fool of you?"

I shouldn't have told her, but I figured she'd know in a few days anyhow. Besides, the rage was cooling and I was the tiniest bit tipsy. It didn't take as much to get me buzzed, thanks to my fancy meds. I explained the kissing game with Sylvie and the experiment. I told her about the girls at Clara's party.

But I didn't tell her about Pilar.

Despite Ballard and Sylvie telling me I wasn't Pilar's boyfriend, I knew Pilar believed I was. I knew from those long text messages with all of their intimate details.

I knew, but I didn't want to know, because I didn't want her to be my girlfriend, and I had no idea how to say so without hurting her feelings.

Girls were too damn complicated.

"So, you are kissing as many girls as you can?" Erin leaned her elbows on her knees, the glass bottle dangling from her fingertips.

"I was. Basically."

"Why?"

"To see if it would calm my tics." I sighed. "It does, but I'm not sure it really matters after all. Do I really want to be with a girl who only likes me when I don't look like I have Tourette's?"

"That's true," Erin says. "But if it works, that is still really cool, right?"

"Yeah, it's cool. I mean, I've wanted to stop my tics for years, and it feels sort of good, ya know? Being still."

"So, you needed to kiss girls to get data for this experiment?"

"Right."

"Well, okay then. I'm game."

It took a minute for her words to register through the fog of my brain. "Wait . . . what?"

"I said, I'm game. You can kiss me. For your experiment."

"No." I said it instantly, no weighing pros and cons needed. I could not kiss Erin Mielke.

"Why not?" I wasn't sure if her voice sounded hurt or surprised.

What I said was, "We're friends. I don't want to ruin that," but what I wanted to say was, *Because you used to have a crush on me forever ago and I never felt that way about you, and if I kiss you, there's a chance I will give you the wrong idea, and besides I am done with this stupid experiment.*

She narrowed her eyes. "Is this about middle school? I know you know I liked you in middle school, but come on, that was forever ago. This is not some bid to steal your heart. You want to kiss a bunch of girls. I'm a girl."

I shook my head and took another beer from her stash. It was against my better judgment to drink it, but I felt awkward and wanted to cover that up. And when she started talking about the experiment again, I was tingly and happy. The stars were so pretty. I lay on my back to stare at them, and Erin lay beside me.

"You think I'm ugly?" Erin asked.

I rolled onto my side and looked at her. "No. That's not it."

"Then kiss me, Stephen. Let's see if it works. You've kicked me twice since I lay down here. I'm sort of curious myself now."

My face pinked, but my lips tingled pleasantly from the beer and I was irrationally annoyed with Pilar, even though Pilar hadn't done anything to deserve my annoyance. What better way to prove I was nobody's boyfriend than to kiss another girl? And it was just Erin. She'd never tell.

"Okay," I said.

We both were still. She took off her glasses and dropped them to her side. I leaned forward and almost fell on top of her. She giggled and sounded like any other high school girl, not so sophisticated after all.

With one arm balancing me, I slowly touched my lips to hers. She tasted slightly sour, like the beer, but it wasn't an entirely unpleasant sensation. She snaked her arms around my neck and I slid my tongue past her teeth. Just as I was going to pull back and end the kiss, there was the sound of laughter, but it wasn't coming from me or Erin.

"Whoa, sorry, man," someone said from the entrance to the tree house.

Before I could make out a face in the dark, the head dropped back out of the entrance.

I sat up and rubbed my eyes. What was I thinking, kissing Erin Mielke?

"I want to know who's up there," a voice said, talking to someone below on the ground. Joan's head appeared in the entrance and she laughed. "Hey, Stephen. Long time no see."

"Sorry," I said. "We'll get out of your way. We were just leaving."

Joan shook her head. "You were not. You were only getting started. You even still have your clothes on."

"It's not like that," I said. It was becoming a mantra for me. The tingle of my beer buzz evaporated, my skin turning clammy.

"It's always the preacher's kid, right? Isn't that how it goes?"

"Come on, Joan," a boy called.

"I'm coming," she answered. "You two stay put. No worries."

And she was gone. The tree house was silent again.

"Are you embarrassed to be caught kissing me?" Erin asked. Her voice was soaked with hurt, and I wanted to punch my own self in the face. Stupid stupid stupid stupid Stephen.

"No," I said. "I just . . ."

But I didn't know what to say next. I just what?

"I need to get home."

"How? You said you came with Ballard?"

She was right. Damn.

"Besides, Josh's parents won't let anyone leave tonight. That's the deal. They buy the booze, but no one is allowed to drive until tomorrow morning. You can go to the house and they'll let you sleep there, but most people stay here by the river. It's not cold out or anything."

I yawned. It had to be nearly morning already. How long had I been drinking with Erin? How long did I spend arguing with Ballard?

"Come on, you can sleep up here with me."

I should've argued, but what was the point? I wasn't going to hike out of the woods to get cell signal and call my parents. I was absolutely not in the mood for a lecture about my "poor choices."

So I laid my head in Erin's lap while she leaned against the wall. Sometime later, I heard voices and a few more people climbed into the tree house. Someone brought blankets and passed them around. A pillow appeared, and I was out again. When the sun rose, I found myself in the corner, arms wrapped around Erin, head throbbing like a drum line.

In the light of day, the night before was like a dream. I left the tree house and caught a ride with a guy from my English class. Neither of us spoke, and he dropped me at the entrance to Lost Bridge Trail. I couldn't go home yet. Not until my headache faded and I rinsed my mouth out. The kid from my English class passed me a stick of gum before I got out of his car. I thanked him and walked a mile or so on the trail to clear my head.

Somehow, I had to go home and face my mother's church cookout and the reality of what an idiot I was turning out to be. The only good news was, I was out of ways to make my own life any worse.

Chapter Twelve

When I walked in the front door, Dad tossed me his car keys and sent me to pick up bags of ice. I took longer than I really needed to buy a few bags of ice at the Quick-Stop. I wasn't hung over. I hadn't drunk enough for that, but I didn't feel like myself either, and a sugary gas station cappuccino seemed like one way to clear the fog from my head. The party dragged behind my brain like toilet paper stuck to my shoe. I kissed Erin Mielke, and Joan Pearson caught me doing it. Okay, so I wasn't kissing Erin when Joan made her way into the tree house, but whichever guy had been with her saw us, so I'm sure she knew.

At home again, I put the ice into coolers and helped Mom fill them with water and soda.

"I thought you were out with Ballard last night," Mom said. "Why didn't he drop you off?"

"I felt like walking." I turned my face away from her while I found some Diet Coke cans in the ice. "I have a lot on my mind."

She wanted to ask me what was on my mind. I could tell from the "mom-talk" look on her face. "Stephen, I know—"

I dropped the lid on the cooler with a loud bang. "So, your new small group thing, you think it will help these people?"

"I know you're trying to change the subject, and I will let you have it this time. We will talk later. And, yes, I think a small group will help. You know how I feel about worship services not being the be-all and end-all of living as a true disciple. Small groups get people to share in new ways, gives them companions on the journey."

I nodded along, the speech a repeat of one I had heard a million times, so my mind was free to juggle Erin and Joan and . . .

Pilar.

Crap. I'd told her I might call the night before.

"You're right, Mom. Friends are important, and I totally forgot to call one of mine. Can we talk later?"

"Of course, go on."

I ducked out of the kitchen and plugged my phone into the charger. When I powered it up, there were no texts. At all.

Did that mean she wasn't mad? Or did it mean she *was* mad?

I needed to ask a girl, but I didn't have one available. I wished I had Sylvie's phone number. I almost opened Twitter and sent her a DM, but I felt like too big of a dork to do that.

I should've texted Pilar right then, but I was already so deep into not doing what I should with Pilar, like being honest with her about my feelings, that I didn't see the point. Instead I lay on my bed and dozed until voices filled the kitchen a couple of hours later. Mom's high-pitched laugh darted down the hallway and through my door. Dad knocked and ordered me up and at 'em.

I almost walked straight into the kitchen, but stopped

in the bathroom to wash my face first, after catching sight of myself in a mirror in the hall. I brushed my teeth while I was at it.

When I finally made it to the group, I was surprised to find Nick Dane and his dad lugging in toolboxes. It turned out the electricity issue needed to be dealt with ASAP, so they were working on Saturday. I knew it had to be driving Mom nuts. You'd be able to hear their tools and their talk while she was hosting a church event.

My second surprise was when I stepped into the backyard and found Joan on the wooden porch swing near the door, arms crossed and lips scowling. Even with a grouchy attitude, she was gorgeous. The green skirt was gone, replaced by skinny jeans and sandals. I stared a little too long.

"What're you looking at?"

"Oh, nothing, sorry." I glanced away and then back at her face. "I was surprised to find you here."

"I'm not staying. I'm waiting on Mom to bring me a Coke."

I nodded. "That's cool. But, I mean, it would be cool if you stayed too." I had no control over my mouth. I sounded like an idiot and I knew it, but I couldn't stop. "I mean, you know, I'm the only teenager here. It'll be sort of boring. But you have plans, right? Somewhere else to be, I mean."

I lost count of how many times the phrase "I mean" tumbled from my lips.

"People were talking about you last night," Joan said, ignoring my babble.

I stared hard at the boards of our deck.

"Don't you want to know what they were saying?"

I shook my head. "Nope. I have a pretty good idea, thanks to Ballard."

"That kid's got a big mouth," Joan pointed out needlessly. "Why do you hang around him so much?"

"He's my best friend," I answered automatically. After he outed my kissing game in front of all of those drunk guys at Josh's party, I wasn't so sure "best friend" was still an accurate title for Ballard Keighley. My rib cage felt tight, and I wanted to cry like I used to, but I also felt angry, and I really wanted to not deal with any of that right then.

"Some friend," Joan said. "Did you have sex with some chick in a mall bathroom?"

My face flamed. "No. I didn't."

It was worse than I'd imagined. I should've known. A rumor isn't any fun unless it gets exaggerated a little more every time it's repeated.

"It didn't really sound like you." Joan scooted over and I sat beside her on the swing. Her mom appeared with a Coke and we made small talk for a few minutes before Mrs. Pearson went back inside to help my mom in the kitchen.

"I should go now." Joan opened her can and took a drink. "I gave Mom a ride, so I'll be back to pick her up after a while."

"Okay," I said. "You're welcome to stay though."

Joan smiled. "Thanks, Stephen."

She didn't get up, though. Instead she pushed the swing back with her legs and let it go. We watched the adults carry food out and arrange it on the picnic table. They said grace while Dad flipped burgers on the grill.

"Wanna get out of here with me?" Joan asked. "We can take my car. Go somewhere without parents. I am so sick of parents."

"Or we could ride to the river," I suggested. "That's where I go when I need to get away from parents."

She frowned. "You mean on the old bike you're always riding? We're a little old for that, don't you think?"

"Nope." I couldn't believe she'd noticed my bike. "Never too old to ride a bicycle. Come on."

I rolled Gwinn the Schwinn out of the garage and met Joan in the driveway. She was leaning against her pink Beetle, and something about her posture reminded me of *Grease*, one of Mom's favorite movies. She was a little like Rizzo, but she was more like the head of the boys' gang with the slick hair and leather jacket. Joan had neither slick hair nor a leather jacket, but it didn't matter. That's how she looked—cool, aloof, and beautiful.

"Y'all having work done?" She nodded toward the yellow truck parked on the street.

"Yeah, they're tearing our house up, adding an office for my dad."

"What's he do?"

I never knew the best answer to that question. Dad's a writer, but he doesn't write novels or anything like what people expect when you tell them your dad's a writer. He used to do safety inspections on chemical plants, and he's sort of a jack-of-all-trades when it comes to fields of study. But calling him a scientist brings up creepy images of bony men in giant goggles cackling over beakers in stainless steel laboratories.

"He writes, mostly," I answered lamely.

"Cool. Writing's cool." Joan nodded absently, still looking at the yellow truck.

I threw a leg over my bike and rolled closer. "You ready to go?"

"I guess." She tore her eyes away from the construction vehicle and examined Gwinn. "We won't both fit."

"Sure we will. You can ride on the handlebars if you want, or else stand behind me, but that may not work as well."

She eyed me dubiously.

"I'm serious. Erin rode on my handlebars once. I didn't wreck her."

"Erin, huh?" Joan smirked.

I remembered Joan peeking into the tree house the night before, my body so close to Erin's, the taste of beer making my stomach roil in regret. "Erin and I are friends. Her dad works at The Exchange."

"Uh-huh." The smirk stayed put.

"Look, are you getting on or not?"

"Fine, but I feel like a twelve-year-old."

It took a few attempts, but once Joan was situated, I took off, pedaling against the wind and letting tics and girlfriends and drunk party hookups fly away behind me. For all of her protesting, Joan enjoyed the ride. Halfway to the river, she laughed, a sort of crazy-sounding laugh that came to me in jolts of sound, not unlike a vocal tic I had in fifth grade.

"What's so funny?" I asked after we locked my bike to a tree near the Tallapoosa. Above us, the huge bridge towered in the afternoon sunlight.

"I don't know." Joan did a sort of spinning dance across the grass, moving downhill toward the water.

No matter how many girls I'd talked to in the last month or so, they still baffled me. "What do you mean, you don't know? Something made you laugh."

"It's everything." She motioned around us.

I didn't see anything funny. Just some trees, grass that would soon turn brown in autumn, big gray rocks along the water's edge.

"I mean, my life is crap, Stephen, real, honest-to-God crap. I live in a shitfest of shittiness, and here I am, right in the middle of all my awfulness, riding on bicycle handlebars with wind in my hair." At the mention of hair, she took a rubber band from her wrist and looped her black hair, creating a messy kind of bun at the nape of her neck.

I had to walk past Joan. The sight of her neck, the slope of it, the creamy skin disappearing beneath her T-shirt . . . my body responded even more obviously to that small gesture than it had when Pilar was pressed against me in the mall bathroom.

My foot jerked out as I made my way down the bank and sat on a boulder. I leaned over, elbows on knees, hiding any lingering signs of where my mind went.

Joan followed and sat beside me.

"So, what everyone was talking about last night . . . is it true?"

I shook my head. "I already told you, no, I never had sex in a bathroom."

"Not that." She knocked her knee against mine, and my elbow dislodged.

I caught myself and sat upright. "Then what?"

"Ballard said you believe kissing girls will treat your Tourette's."

I rolled my eyes. "Ballard's an idiot."

"Isn't he your best friend?"

"He is my best friend, but that doesn't make him any less of an idiot."

"So you don't need to kiss me right now?"

I opened and closed my mouth, completely unable to form words. I'd have liked to kiss Joan, but not as part of some dumb experiment. But I also didn't want her to know I wanted to kiss her. Joan was clearly still in love with Wade, and God only knew who the boy in the tree house had been.

"So, no experiment?"

A lock of dark hair came loose from her bun. It fluttered across her face in the wind, and I tucked it behind her ear. The gesture was small, but I'd seen it done by a billion men in a billion of Mom's old movies, so I knew it could be construed as romantic.

I glanced away, even as my fingers brushed her cheekbone. Just as the curve of Joan's neck affected me earlier, the warmth of her skin shot through me faster than the beer I should've never drunk. I'd rather have touched Joan's face one more time than slide my hand inside Pilar's shirt again and again and again. That was the data I needed to analyze, not my reaction to kissing, but my reaction to Joan.

"Why is your life a shitfest?" I asked.

She caught my fingers with her own, holding our hands

suspended between us. "Why did you want to get out of your house so badly last night?"

"I asked first," I said.

"Nope." She shook her head. "I asked you last night, and you refused to answer. You first."

I chuckled. "Fine. There's this girl, and I may have screwed things up with her."

"What'd you do?" She lowered our hands, but our fingers stayed entwined.

I considered possible answers to her question. Because I wasn't entirely sure what I'd done, other than follow Pilar blindly through the mall and through whatever kind of relationship she believed we were in. It was too long of a story to explain.

I went with the reason Pilar was mad at me right that second. "I didn't call when I said I would."

"Is that all?" Joan nudged my leg with hers again. "That's easy to solve."

"Easy how?"

"Apologize. Acknowledge you screwed up and promise not to do it again." Untangling our fingers, Joan leaned back on her elbows.

I wasn't sure Joan's advice fit my situation. I couldn't decide if I wanted to make up with Pilar. "Your turn. Explain the shitfest."

"You remember my sister? Pearl?"

I nodded.

"Well, she's been away at college, and she got married. Without telling anyone. Mom found out on Facebook."

“Wow.” There wasn’t much else to say.

“Yeah, and Dad lost his job. Pearl says that’s why she didn’t tell anyone, because she knew we couldn’t afford a wedding right now, but no one believes her. She married this guy we met once, and no one liked him. She didn’t want us to talk her out of it.”

Joan didn’t volunteer any more information, but the look on her face screamed fear and bitterness. I might have pressed the issue, but the clouds were darkening and the wind was picking up. I knew we needed to leave right away if we wanted to get back to the house before the rain moved in. So I helped Joan navigate the rocks back to the grassy bank and we made our way to my bike, Gwinn’s green paint glistening in the pre-storm light.

“I’m glad you brought us here instead of over the bridge.” Joan waited while I unlocked Gwinn’s two locks.

“Why? What’s wrong with the bridge?” Lots of kids liked to hang out on the bridge. There are sidewalks on either side, and tall fencing the town council had erected after an attempted suicide three years ago.

She shaded her eyes and looked over the looming concrete structure. “Have you ever been terrified of something you couldn’t explain?”

“Sure,” I said.

“I’m like that with bridges,” she said. “I can’t stand them.”

Something about her words dislodged a memory . . . the last day of summer vacation, standing on the bridge, holding my proud middle finger in the air as Joan flew by, knuckles white on her steering wheel. Maybe she hadn’t been pissed off at Wade. Maybe what I saw on her face that day wasn't anger.

Maybe it was fear.

The next morning, I got to church early because I'd promised Matt I'd help set up chairs in the youth area. They'd used the space for a kid's birthday party over the weekend, and there were still scattered balloons and streamers to be cleared away. Matt ran the vacuum over the carpeted areas while I arranged chairs.

When Erin came in, the roaring of the Hoover eliminated the awkwardness of a forced conversation. She helped me with the chairs and, as I passed her to go to the little kids' class, she reached out and touched my arm. The vacuum stopped. I paused, breathed in quick, kicked out hard enough to hurt my toe when my foot hit the wall, but I didn't yelp with pain or mutter a curse word. I held it in, more worried about what Erin might want from me than what my foot was doing.

"We're cool, right?" Erin's thin lips were cracked, dry. "I mean, Friday night . . . I was drunk, and I was upset about Miles and—"

"Yeah, we're cool." I was relieved. That could've been bad.

"I saw you, yesterday, by the river with Joan Pearson." Erin held me in place with one hand. My big toe throbbed. "You shouldn't hang around Joan."

"What do you mean, you saw me?" I jerked my arm from her grip.

She shook her head. "I was here, helping with the birthday party. You can see the bridge and all from upstairs, you know."

Yeah, I knew, but we weren't supposed to go upstairs.

"I was hung over. I needed to hide from Dad for a bit." She twisted her hands together, the long fingers fluttering in my periphery.

"Why do you care?" I put my hand on the doorknob, ready to walk away.

"Joan's bad news, Stephen. She's always drunk, or worse, and people are saying she . . ." Erin's face was crimson. She didn't want to finish her sentence, but I wasn't about to let her off that easy. If she wanted to warn me away from Joan, she better have more to say than "Joan drinks."

"People are saying she what? Because you were plastered Friday night, and that means you can't judge anyone else for drinking."

Erin gritted her teeth before answering. "People are saying she's a slut."

"What in the world do you think you saw from the upstairs window? I can guarantee it wasn't sex." I opened the door but kept glaring at Erin, so self-righteous, standing there in the youth room, holding her hot pink Bible under one arm, such a good little church girl. "I've heard things about you too, Erin, about you at certain college parties with certain college boys who like to brag about what they can make a high school girl do once they get a few beers in her."

I was lying. I wanted to defend Joan and made up stories about Erin to let Joan off the hook. My foot kicked out twice and I grimaced.

Tears sparked in Erin's eyes. How do girls do that? Insta-cry. It's a superpower.

"I've never . . ." She paused to wipe her eyes. "I'm a virgin. I'm waiting until I'm married, like you're supposed to be."

"Look, Erin, I get that, okay, but you can't expect us all to feel exactly as you do."

"What are you saying, Stephen? This experiment . . . are you just kissing all these girls? What would've happened if we hadn't been interrupted in the tree house? I was drunk and emotional and you never should've kissed me. Would you have pushed it further if no one found us? 'Cause people were talking about you Saturday, and I chose not to believe them. I told them I know Stephen Luckie and he would never have sex with a girl at all, let alone in a mall bathroom."

I shook my head. "Believe what you want."

It is frustrating to say words that make sense in your head but have no one understand them. How many ways could I tell Erin to move on without being even ruder? I hate when I can't make someone understand me, and I hate being stuck in a situation I don't know the answer to.

So I left her there. Yes, I left a crying girl I had basically called a slut all alone. Well, not exactly alone. Matt was there. Her youth minister. The kind of person a teenager can talk to about anything. The kind of person a good Christian girl might tell when she's scared the preacher's son is in trouble.

My mind stayed on Erin long after I left the youth room. For the second time in a weekend, rage vibrated in my toes and moved through my body. My leg jerked and my shoulder followed suit. I didn't go to the kids' area of the church. Instead, I went straight home and into the garage, where my mother had hung a punching bag in seventh grade. I hadn't used it in ages. When I threw the first punch, dust flew and I sneezed.

My mistake wasn't leaving Erin to talk things over with Matt. My mistake was saying those stupid mean things to her. My mistake was letting her talk me into beer and kissing, the sour lukewarm taste of one confused with the other, making my hands sweat in the moment and at the memory.

I knew Erin had a certain image of me, and it didn't matter if she didn't even live up to that perfect Christian image herself. My mom was the pastor, and I was supposed to be perfect. It was an age-old cliché, the preacher's kid who could do no wrong and also did everything wrong. My chest was tight with it, the certainty I'd screw up again, the fear of where my mistakes would take me.

I punched the bag hard, again and again, until my muscles ached and tears poured down my cheeks.

I pulled out my phone and texted Erin, *I'm sorry.*

But it was too late.

Chapter Thirteen

People looked at me differently on Monday. I walked through the halls with my leg jerking so hard I kicked lockers, and one teacher yelled at me to stop it before she realized who I was. She stammered out an apology, but whatever. It was kind of nice to get yelled at for my tics.

I know, that sounds stupid, but the truth is, my kicking things and shrugging twenty-four freaking seven is annoying. It annoys me, but I can't do much about it. It annoys my mother. I watch her bite her lip sometimes, steeling her spine for the next twitch sure to follow, but she won't say a word. Not since this one time, in sixth grade, when she snapped at me over a vocal tic that made me sound like a stuttering Spanish actor, constantly rolling my *R*s.

People get annoyed by my flapping and flailing, but they're too polite or compassionate or maybe too scared to say anything about it. So, despite the evil glare I tossed in the teacher's direction, I wasn't mad at her.

I *was* mad at Ballard.

He met me in the parking lot looking sheepish. I locked Gwinn to the bike rack and he tried to help me with the second lock.

"Don't," I snapped. "Just don't."

"I'm sorry, man. I was drunk."

I popped the second lock into place and stood. "Not my problem, Ballard. If you can't be a decent human being when you're drunk, maybe you shouldn't spend so much time getting drunk."

"Sheesh, Luckie. Self-righteous, much?"

I didn't answer, just pushed past him and headed to class. All of the way there, people whispered. Then there was the teacher who yelled, and I was in Chemistry, not looking at anyone and not talking, copying notes with my jaw set hard and my foot repeatedly kicking the leg of my desk.

At lunch, I figured I'd sit by myself, but it didn't turn out that way. I avoided the table where Ballard sat, talking to Sylvie. Michael and Joel were there, and Andrew. It looked a lot like the circle on the lake house deck at the last party of the summer. I remembered the phone being passed around and me following Sylvie up the stairs into that bedroom, tripping over Barbies. It had been less than two months, but my life felt like somebody else's.

"There goes the mad scientist," Wade said when I passed his table. My spine stiffened, but I ignored him.

I was sitting in a back corner of the cafeteria, eating a brownie without even tasting it, when Joan sat down.

"Sure you want to be seen with me?" I asked.

"You already told me the rumors aren't true." She broke off a piece of the brownie in my hand, her fingers cool against my own. "Gah, this is delicious. Did your mom make these?"

I nodded. "I only said the sex in the bathroom rumor isn't

true. The stupid experiment is real, though it was Ballard's damn idea in the first place."

She licked chocolate crumbs off her fingers. I tried not to stare.

"Why aren't you sitting with Wade? Or Sylvie?"

"Wade's being an asshole and Sylvie's occupied."

I glanced at their table. "By Ballard, you mean? You and I both know he's getting nowhere with her."

"You may know that, but I don't." Joan took the rest of my brownie and popped it into her mouth. Bits of chocolate stuck to her glossy lips.

"You think Ballard has a shot with Sylvie?"

She finished chewing before she answered. "Not normally, but Sylvie's acting odd lately. She broke up with her boyfriend and keeps talking about 'living the high school experience.' That's where the kissing game app came in. But no one else knows about the breakup, okay? Don't say anything."

"Who would I tell? People are too busy talking *about me* to listen *to me*." I handed her a napkin and she dabbed her lips. I watched, eyes glued to the motion of her mouth.

"Quit staring. It's rude." She stood.

"Sorry, I—"

"I'm kidding, Stephen. I have to go to the library. Wanna come?"

I bagged the rest of my lunch and followed her out of the cafeteria. We didn't talk anymore, not about the rumors or Ballard or Sylvie, at least. We quizzed each other on notes for Tuesday's Algebra II test, and she told me our bike ride had inspired her to pull out her old bicycle, but she'd outgrown it.

"I'll keep my eyes open for a bike when I hit the thrift store this week. That's where I found mine."

"No way," she said. "You thrift?"

Talk about embarrassing. Thrift shopping was decidedly uncool.

"I'm always in the thrift store downtown, but I never see you there. That place is my favorite. I find the neatest things. We should go together."

Definitely not a date . . . not to the thrift store . . . but I liked the idea of hanging out with Joan and doing something I enjoyed. No parties. No beers. No being spied on from the church's upstairs windows.

"I was gonna go tomorrow, after school," I told her. "You can come too if you want."

"Perfect. I can't go right after, but I could meet you at, say, four thirty?"

"That'll work."

My phone buzzed in my pocket. I had a text from an unfamiliar number.

This is Pilar using Isabel's phone. I'm not mad anymore, and I'm sorry for ignoring your texts all weekend. You are allowed to go to parties. I wish I could have gone with you.

Okay. What else was I supposed to say?

Can I see you soon? You could come here over the weekend.

I don't know. I stared at the phone, unsure of myself. I knew I needed to end things with Pilar. I wasn't as into her as she was into me. All of those conversations we'd had on iMessage, the things she shared and I shared back. We were acting like boyfriend and girlfriend, and stringing her along wasn't fair. But I was scared. What if no girl ever liked me again?

My parents are visiting family in Georgia. I can't go because I have to study. You could quiz me.

If I ignored the part about her parents not being home, it sounded innocent. If I went, then I could be honest with Pilar in person. You weren't supposed to give someone bad news over text message, right?

Maybe. I'll ask to borrow the car.

She sent back a smiley emoticon.

"Intense conversation?" Joan asked.

On Saturday when I talked to Joan, I hadn't explained everything about Pilar. But it was quiet in the library, and the look on Joan's face was interested but not smirky, like the kids whispering in the hall that morning.

"That girl I told you about, Pilar? She wants me to come over this weekend since her parents won't be there."

"The girl you didn't call?"

I nodded.

"Nuh-uh, Stephen." She shook her head, black hair dancing on her shoulders. "If you don't want to be with this girl, tell her so. Going to her house when her parents aren't home does not send a not-interested message."

"I don't want to tell her over the phone."

"Sounds like an excuse to me. A horny boy making an excuse so he can get some before he ditches the girl." Joan's glare cut me open. I didn't consciously plan to do that, but maybe it is what I was doing.

"Meet her somewhere else, somewhere public," Joan told me. "Text her right now."

"Sheesh, Miss Bossypants, hang on." I unlocked my phone and suggested Pilar meet me somewhere to study, a coffee shop maybe.

She didn't answer and the bell rang, sending Joan and me on our way to English, which we also had together.

"Text me when she answers, okay?" Joan slid into her seat near the front of the classroom.

"I will." My feet were surer of their steps with Joan's support and advice. I was going to do the right thing. If only I could channel that confidence into the report I had to give that afternoon. If I let my grades flounder, Mom and Dad would step in. Then the little bit of a social life I was beginning to build would crumble.

My oral report on *Gatsby* was due, and I had to stay after school to give it. My 504 plan allowed for that, so I didn't have to talk in front of the entire class. I was still a nervous wreck.

As soon as I stood, my tongue did a flip. It's my most hated tic, where my tongue flicks and it makes a spitty sort of sound. I look like a snake or a lizard when it happens, and it almost always happens when I'm in front of people.

If the tics continued this severely, I'd have to tell Mom and go to the neurologist. I'd put on enough weight since my last med change to possibly warrant a dose increase. I really hated trying new medications. Some had nasty side effects and made me feel like a zombie. I felt a little sick to my stomach thinking about another round of medication trial and error.

I got through the report only barely and left the classroom

with my teeth clenched in an effort to end the tongue flipping. I was passing the entrance to Coach Curry's office when the shouting started. I would've kept walking, but I caught a glimpse of Wade from the corner of my eye. I did a double take and took three steps back, so I could see through the window.

Sure enough, Wade was getting yelled at. His head was in his hands, but then he looked up, probably at Coach Curry, and I forgot to clench my teeth. Flick flick flick went my tongue, but the coach was screaming so loud, no way they heard it. I moved away from the window and paused by a locker to re-clench my teeth and process what I'd seen.

Wade Bond.

Crying.

No effing way.

Coach Curry's voice rang through the door, so I left the school knowing full well why Wade was getting a new asshole ripped into him. He was failing a class. A math class. We need four math credits to graduate, so failing was bad. Not to mention, a failing grade next to Wade's barely average GPA (according to Coach) meant he was about to sit the bench the rest of this season. And lose the chance at a scholarship, though that part didn't seem like a big deal. Wade's parents were loaded.

When the yelling stopped, I hightailed it out of there before Wade found me eavesdropping. I passed his silver Lexus in the senior lot on my way to the bike rack. I unlocked both of Gwinn the Schwinn's locks and pedaled fast. No way did I want to be anywhere near when Wade made it to his car and drove home. He'd pass me on my bike, and I wasn't up to taking the beating he wanted to hand to Coach.

When I walked through the front door, Mom was waiting at the kitchen table. Her face was drawn, her lips tight. Dad walked out of his office and sat beside her, motioning for me to take the chair across from them.

"Someone came to my office today, someone with an interesting story about you, Stephen. I wanted to not believe this story. It sounded nothing like the young man we raised. However, the source is reliable."

"Erin," I said. "Shit."

"Watch your language," Dad warned.

"Erin went to your office? During school?"

"No, she didn't. She went to someone else and that person came to my office, but how the whole thing landed in my lap doesn't matter. Since you know who told in the first place, I'm guessing I'm right to believe her."

"No," I snapped. "Erin accused me of some things Sunday, and they aren't true. She got it wrong. She's not some perfect angel like you think she is."

"Erin was honest about her role in some of the activities. I know she was drinking with you at a party Friday night. Are you saying this is untrue?" Mom's hands were pressed together hard.

My mother doesn't lose her temper. Ever. But I can tell when she's angry, because she trembles. She was trying her best to hide the quiver in her muscles, but I could spot it a mile away. And, once again, I was the cause of a mother-quake.

"That part's true," I admitted.

"You told us you were going to Ballard's house. You lied, Stephen."

"I'm sorry. I really am, but—"

"Sorry isn't enough. Lying is unacceptable. Let's talk about the rest of Erin's story."

"She's mad at me, Mom. She's mad and she did this to get back at me. I knew I shouldn't have kissed her."

"You kissed Erin Mielke?" Dad raised an eyebrow.

I nodded.

Dad tried not to smile. Talk about flipping roles on me. Here Mom was, pissed as hell, and Dad was the quiet one.

"Can we talk about this later? I have homework."

"No, we can't, and you will have plenty of time to do your homework. Trust me. Plenty of time."

"Am I grounded?"

"I'm asking the questions here." Mom leaned onto the table and looked at me. "Stephen, I need you to be honest with me."

"I'm always honest with you." I ducked my head. "Okay, I'm usually honest with you. I knew you'd say no to the party and I wasn't planning to drink or do anything stupid."

"Stephen, are you having sex?"

"With Erin?"

"With anyone," Dad amended.

"No. I'm not." I stood up from the table. They were acting like I'd committed murder by going to a party and kissing a girl.

"Erin said—"

"I know what Erin said, Mom, and it's Ballard who

started that rumor. I did not have sex with anyone anywhere, and especially not in some dirty mall bathroom. I can't believe you are even asking me this crap." My arms shook from my shoulders to my fists.

I inherited Mom's quivering anger mixed with Dad's shouting rage, though Dad controls his way better than I do.

Mom sighed. "Why would Ballard say such a thing?"

"Because he was drunk. He was drunk and I was teasing him, and he couldn't take being the one people laughed at. He had to turn it back on me." I backed away from my parents, fists clenched and breath coming harder and harder. This is how it always started, with me trying to be understood. I didn't want much, just to be understood.

Mom watched me. She recognized the signs, my labored breathing and the way my shoulders shook. "Stephen, take a deep breath. Count to ten."

"I don't want to fucking count to ten," I growled at her, light flashing oddly before my eyes. My head was swimmy, not like Friday with the beer making me tipsy. When I get angry, really angry, my head fills with someone I don't recognize and my brain has to fight to keep that other person out of me.

"Stephen Luckie, don't you dare speak to your mother that way." Dad stood and took a step around the table. "You have no right to be angry with us for something you've done to yourself."

It was his usual spiel, telling me I didn't have the right to feel my feelings. He was wrong though. Maybe I didn't have the right to shout at my mother or throw things, but I did have a right to be angry.

"You don't understand. You aren't listening to me." The room spun.

"I do understand. I understand you lied to us and went to a party where you knew there would be drinking and who knows what else, and while there you got drunk and took advantage of the situation with a young lady who is dear to our family." The my-son-kissed-a-girl pride was gone from his voice.

"That's not what happened." I clenched my teeth. The room spun faster.

"It is exactly what you just told us happened."

He'd twisted it. He'd twisted what I said, what I admitted to. I did not take advantage of Erin. I went to the party. I drank. I kissed her, but it was her idea, not mine. She took advantage of me, if anything. She handed me the beer. She asked me to kiss her.

"It's about time you grow up and take responsibility for your actions, Stephen. You have to quit using your Tourette's as a crutch."

I don't even remember picking it up. One minute, Dad was lecturing, his voice rising, and the next, I was screaming and a saltshaker was flying across the room. It hit the wall near my mother's head and bounced to the floor.

The rage drained out of me. I looked at my outstretched hand, my eyes on the indentations from gripping the rose-shaped saltshaker, its red petals and green leaves now shattered on the tile floor. Mom's face was white.

I didn't wait for further reprimand. I ran down the hall and locked myself inside my bedroom. Through the wall there were hammers and men's voices. I supposed the construction crew heard everything. I pictured Nick Dane, smoking his cigarette, telling his buddies about the family feud at the Luckie house that afternoon.

"Stephen?" Mom knocked on the door.

I didn't answer, just pressed my back against the wood. It was all so eerily familiar, my sitting like this, the carpet thick beneath me, the door thin, the sound of Mom breathing on the other side.

I didn't hit her though. The saltshaker busted against the floor. It only hit the wall, and Mom was wearing shoes this time. So she didn't step in the glass.

Minutes passed. I sensed Mom's weight against the door and heard her sliding to a seat. For a little while, we sat like that. Then, slowly, I inched my fingers under the door. Sure enough, Mom's hand was there, waiting.

Chapter Fourteen

Tuesday, I canceled thrift store plans with Joan. I had no choice. I was grounded for two weeks. I didn't cancel on Pilar though. I knew I should, but I had high hopes of getting time off for good behavior. I wanted to go study with a friend, right? There was no party. There would be no alcohol.

Tuesday night, after dinner, I was working on a paper for English. My phone was turned off and locked in a drawer in Dad's desk, but I still had access to iMessage on my Mac. My parents both used ancient PCs, so this didn't occur to them, and I wasn't about to point it out.

Joan had gone to the thrift store without me and sent a message to say there were no bikes in stock this week. I promised to take her for a ride again when I got out of prison. *I'll break you out*, she replied.

Please do, I wrote back.

A car pulled into the drive and for a second I thought Joan was magic. It wasn't Joan though.

"Knock, knock," Matt said, stepping through my open bedroom door.

I snapped my Mac closed and crossed my arms.

"Your mom said you might need someone to talk to. I hear it's been a tough weekend."

"Thanks to you." No way was I going to bare my soul to Matt. I knew good and well he was Erin's confidant, and he turned around and handed me over to my mother. I get it, she's his boss, but he's supposed to be someone I can trust. Before this, I did trust him. He's the only nonfamily member who knows I want to write songs. He and I stayed up till three in the morning talking on youth trips. How could he automatically believe Erin and tattle on me?

Matt sat on the edge of my bed, brow knit seriously. "I didn't know anything about it before today. Am I missing a detail?"

"How can you even pretend that's true? When I left Sunday morning, who was with Erin? You."

Matt folded his hands and went quiet for a minute, then spoke. "Erin hasn't said a word to me. You're right about her being upset Sunday morning, but she didn't want to speak with me. She talked to Kelly instead."

"So your wife turned me in. Same difference."

"Not quite. I didn't even know this is what Erin was upset about. Can you cut me a little slack, buddy?"

"Please don't call me 'buddy.' I'm not twelve."

Matt nodded slowly. "I know rumors get blown out of proportion in high school. I've been there, and not too long ago."

Matt was only twenty-five. He liked to remind us of that pretty often. Kelly's even younger.

"Whatever." I reopened the Mac and pretended to focus on the screen.

"Okay, then. Well, your parents are going out of town

this weekend, for a conference, and I said you could stay with us."

That was news to me. "I can stay here. I'm old enough to take care of myself."

"Your mother said the same, but you are still grounded, so we needed a compromise. You can stay by yourself so long as you check in with me every few hours, and you come to our house for dinner Saturday. Deal?"

"Fine, whatever. Please go now."

He left me alone with my thoughts and the glowing laptop screen. I couldn't stay mad at Matt for something he didn't do. I'd apologize for my grouchiness later. In the meantime, at least my parents still trusted me enough to leave me home alone. Checking in with Matt was better than staying at his house under Kelly's watchful eye.

By Friday, with no word from Pilar about my coffee shop suggestion, I'd decided not to go at all. Joan was right. If I went to Pilar's house when her parents weren't home, there's no telling what would happen. Besides, Dad left his car parked in the driveway instead of the garage. I had keys in case of an emergency, but if I took the car, Matt would know. He and Kelly lived three doors down.

I texted Pilar in the morning and told her I couldn't make it. When I joined Joan in the library at lunch, I still hadn't gotten a reply.

"Let's do something this weekend. Your parents aren't around. I'll pick you up." We were proofreading each other's English essays. Joan had written about Daisy in *The Great*

Gatsby, about how being a "beautiful little fool" sounded like a fate worse than death. She said her sister, Pearl, was a beautiful little fool.

"I can't. Matt might see you pick me up. Or he might call or knock on the door. The whole thing's stupid." I passed Joan's laptop to her, typos corrected.

She handed me mine, an essay about the similarities between Jay Gatsby and Jay-Z. "I'll come over. I'll sneak in the back. I've gotta get out of my house tomorrow. Pearl's home."

"Did she bring the new husband?"

"No, thank God. But she did bring news." Joan closed her MacBook and slid it into her backpack.

"News?"

"She's pregnant."

"Oh." I wasn't sure what the proper response was. "Well, yeah, come over if you want. You can help me figure out what to say to Pilar."

"Sure. We can write you a script." She smiled at me, her eyes bright but not entirely happy.

There was a girl at the table next to us. I noticed her as we passed, headed for English, Joan trying to explain the importance of the color yellow in the *Gatsby* narrative. I remember because the girl at the table had on a yellow dress, and when I looked at her, she ducked her head. Her hair fell over her face as she typed away furiously on her laptop. I followed Joan out of the library.

On Saturday, Joan crawled over the back fence and dropped onto the ground in my yard, her pink Converse high-tops bright against the dying grass. That's how she landed in my life too, quick and smooth, suddenly my friend instead of the girl who defended me in seventh grade when I didn't want her to.

After she grabbed snacks from the kitchen, Joan's eyes alighted on the guitar in my bedroom. "Stephen! You play guitar? Play something?"

My heart scattered its beats all over my chest, tossing a few into my throat for good measure. I lifted the guitar and spent a few moments twisting the tuning pegs so I had time to get my nerves under control. At the opening chords of "Hey There Delilah," she smiled, and I was glad she recognized the Plain White T's. It's one of the first songs I learned all the way through.

"Here." I held out the guitar and she took it. I showed her how to pick out three chords, nudging over to where the morning sun shone through my bedroom window and illuminated the strings. My fingers curled around hers on the neck of the guitar. The simple touch made my whole body turn to jelly. My hands itched to do it again, to wrap around her hands and her arms . . . to lead me closer and closer until I could touch every lethal part of Joan Pearson.

Lethal, because that's what a girl like Joan is—a girl I couldn't have.

When I messaged Pilar Friday morning and told her I couldn't come, she took a while to respond, but when she did, she seemed okay with me canceling. I told her I was grounded because of drinking at a party, and that's true. I didn't tell her

I wouldn't have driven to Dadeville even if I wasn't grounded. There was no reason to upset her.

Joan was going to help me figure out how to extricate myself from my might-be-a-relationship with Pilar, and I would drive to Dadeville then. I wasn't a break-up-with-her-via-text-message kind of bastard. I would man up and do it face-to-face.

At lunch, I made sandwiches and flipped on the TV. "There's a *Doctor Who* marathon on BBC America."

"I've never watched it," Joan said.

"Well, then you have to start with the ninth doctor, not the newer seasons." I grabbed the DVDs from a shelf and put the first one in the player. We ate on the couch and then split a bowl of popcorn with white chocolate, something my dad showed me how to make.

"This is so good." Joan reached for another handful and we had one of those movie moments when our fingers brushed, except our hands were sticky from the melted chocolate. When her fingers pulled away from mine and she put those same fingers in her mouth, dropping kernels onto the couch, my body froze and so did my brain.

I forced my eyes to return to the television screen, the breath in my lungs struggling to get out.

It was early evening when Nick Dane arrived. Joan hid in my bedroom while I answered the door. I spotted Matt checking his mail, or pretending to at least. He waved, and I waved so he could report to Mom I was home.

"Hey, man," Nick said when I let him in the house. "I left some tools I need. Mind if I dig around for them?"

I led him down the hall and watched him disappear past the tarps into the in-progress office and bathroom area. Everything smelled of sawdust.

I was pretty sure Nick hadn't forgotten any tools, because when I peeked around the corner a few minutes later, he was sitting with his eyes closed, a joint pinched between two fingers. I didn't ask him to put it out. I was still pissed about being grounded, so I didn't feel like defending my mother or keeping her rules. Besides, she hadn't expressly forbidden me to allow one of the construction workers to get high in our house.

"So, Nick Dane is smoking pot in the add-on," I told Joan, closing the door behind me.

Joan laughed. "That's the least weird place Nick has gotten high."

"You know him, right? I remember he used to drive you to school sometimes." My leg jerked, my foot knocking against my desk.

"Yeah, he lives next door. We hang out sometimes." Joan watched as my foot jerked again. "Come sit before you break something."

I sat on the bed where Joan had a box of my CDs. She popped one into the player on my nightstand and James Durbin's voice filled the room.

"Who's this guy?" Joan turned the case over in her hands.

"He was on *American Idol.* He didn't win, but he came close. And he has Tourette's, so I was into him for a while."

"Is this his signature?" Joan pointed at the thick black cursive scrolled across the booklet that came with the CD.

"Mom mailed it to him, and his wife wrote us a letter when they sent it back signed. That's when I learned to play guitar."

"How come you don't play in the band at The Exchange?" Joan dropped the case into the box and set it aside. When she leaned back again, her hair fell onto my shoulder. It tickled my neck, but I didn't brush it away. "I mean, you're there all the time, and I hear they're pretty good."

"I don't like being on stage or in front of people." It was easy to talk to Joan this way, sitting side by side, looking straight ahead, no eye contact. I could tell her anything.

My shoulder jerked and her hair slipped away, the tickling sensation gone, but the memory of it engraved on my skin. "It stresses me out and I've got this vocal tic, a coughing, throat clearing kind of thing. I hate it."

"But, when you were playing earlier, you didn't tic at all. Not once." She turned her head to look at me and I met her eyes, certain I was going to kiss her. A couple of inches closer, and I would do it. I would take a risk and kiss Joan. I didn't even register what she'd said, her voice quiet against drums pounding from the speakers.

I put aside my grudge against God long enough to say one prayer, a quick plea he would keep my face from grimacing while we were this close, while her eyes were so intensely staring. Let my face hold still while I lean forward . . .

My bedroom door flew open. Joan jerked backward, cold air rushing between us, and we both turned.

"Pilar?" What the hell? I couldn't make sense of her standing there, like some sort of guilty nightmare.

"I knew it," she said. "I didn't want to believe Luz when she said you were all over some girl in the library, but she was right. She was right!"

"What—"

"I told her she didn't know what she was talking about, that you're a good guy, a nice guy, not the kind of guy who cheats."

I stood and crossed the room, but Pilar wouldn't let me talk.

"No, I'm not finished. You listen to me, Stephen." She glanced at Joan and her eyes widened. "Wait a minute. I know her. She's the girl from the mall."

"The mall?" Joan's forehead wrinkled in confusion.

"Yes, you were at the mall when we were, and Stephen was watching you, and I asked if he knew you." Pilar turned back to me. "You called her a bitch. You said she was some bitch."

"That's not what I said." My skin turned clammy. My eyes darted between the two girls in my bedroom.

Joan stood, shot me a dirty look, and left the room. I poked my head out the door and watched Joan disappear behind the tarp, into the construction area where Nick had gone earlier. I wanted to call after her, but I knew it was pointless. I'd have to explain, but I couldn't do that, or anything else, until I faced Pilar. There was no reason for Joan to suffer Pilar's wrath when she hadn't done anything wrong.

"How could you, Stephen?" Pilar dropped her wildly flailing arms and let her voice lower in volume. The quiet was worse. The hurt in her brown eyes stung like a slap.

I turned my back on her, walking across the room and peeking out the window. No sign of Matt, but there was Isabel's silver car parked in the driveway. If Matt spotted it, I'd be in deep shit.

"I was so stupid. Stupid, stupid, stupid, believing your innocent act was the real deal, like, oh, Stephen is so modest and Stephen is so kind, and Stephen isn't like those other guys. Stupid!" Her hands were moving again, making intricate designs in the air.

"If you're referring to Joan, stop. We're just friends. I swear."

"Right. You lied about being grounded this weekend to get out of visiting me, but you have her over here in your friggin' bedroom, and I am supposed to believe anything you say?"

"First of all, I didn't lie. I *am* grounded." My mouth twisted.

Pilar mimicked the twist. God, that hurt. It didn't matter if I'd been planning on ending things with her. It didn't matter if I didn't feel about her how she felt about me. It hurt for someone I trusted to stand there and make fun of me. Tears pushed at my eyes, but I ignored them, choosing to focus on the anger instead.

"How did you even know where I live? And you broke into my house! What kind of person does that? Have you been stalking me? I knew all of this was too fast. I knew I needed to slow it down." My shoulder jerked three times and I grimaced again.

She didn't copy me that time. "I'm not stalking you. I

know your parents' names, remember? I know how to use the effing internet. Your address is available for anyone who wants it. I didn't dig through your trash, you stupid jerk. And I didn't have to break in. I knocked three times before I tried the door. It wasn't locked."

We glared at each other, both of us breathing hard, me fighting the rage, remembering the saltshaker flying past Mom's head a few nights before. I would never be the kind of guy who hits a girl. I would never be a bully.

Pilar started crying. Her face was red and she pressed her hands against her eyes.

"Pilar." I took a step forward.

"Don't touch me. I knew you were too good to be true."

"Pilar," I said again. "I was never your boyfriend. I didn't cheat on you. I couldn't cheat on you, because we were not together . . . not like that."

"Yes, we were. What are you talking about?" Her eyes widened and she rubbed at the tears with her hands.

"No, we never talked about it. You assumed, and I didn't correct you, so that's on me, but Sylvie said—"

"Sylvie? Who the fuck is Sylvie?"

"She's this girl I know—"

"The one that was here?" Pilar's eyes darted toward the hall where Joan had disappeared.

"No, that's Joan. I already told you."

"Joan is the girl Luz saw you with in the library, then. Luz said she was Asian and had a bad dye job."

"Who is Luz? And Joan's hair is fine. Leave her alone."

"Luz is my cousin. She goes to your school, you douchebag.

She saw you with Joan, and she said everyone in Moorhen knows about me, that they all think I slept with you. And she said you screwed some other girl at a party, but I didn't believe her. I didn't *want* to believe her, I mean, but she said she heard it from your friends at school. She heard we had sex at the mall. I can't believe you would let people believe—"

"I didn't. I didn't let people believe anything. Ballard started that rumor, and I couldn't stop it. I kept telling people it wasn't true. I promise, I denied it to everyone I could." My leg kicked out twice, bumping my guitar case. I winced, hoping I hadn't hurt it.

"So what? I'm supposed to take your word for it? I'm supposed to forgive you, just like that, and take you back?" Pilar held out her arms, a gesture somewhere between a question and an invitation.

I shook my head and backed away, dropping onto the bed.

"Answer me, Stephen." She let her arms fall and stood there, looking suddenly weak, not at all like the fiery girl who whirred through my life like a tiny Tasmanian devil.

I made myself meet her eyes. Earlier, I had decided to end things. I planned to do it face-to-face, and here we were, face-to-face.

"Fine, Pilar." I looked at my hands and back at her, the first girl to want me in a way I desperately ached to be wanted. At that moment, I wavered. I wanted so badly to kiss her one last time, to carve her body into my brain, so I could pull out the memory on bad nights. I wanted to always remember how it felt to be wanted.

"Well, answer me."

"I don't feel that way about you . . . the way you feel about me. It was all too fast, and I was a little scared of you."

"You were scared of me?" A strangled laugh escaped her lips.

"I liked you, Pilar. Or, I tried to like you. I enjoyed kissing you, and you have to know how gorgeous you are. It wasn't you—"

"Don't you dare try that washed-up 'it's not you, it's me' shit, Stephen. Tell the truth this time."

"It is the truth." I held out my hands, palms up, offering nothing. "I liked you liking me, more than I actually liked you."

She wiped her eyes and nodded. "Fine, whatever. I have to go. Isabel's waiting."

I walked behind her down the hall. When I opened the front door, Pilar walked out and Matt walked in. He didn't say anything, just watched Pilar walk stiff-spined across the yard and open the passenger door of the silver car. He closed the door once they'd pulled out of the driveway.

"I didn't invite her. I know I'm grounded." I said those words calm as anything, but inside I was quaking. Right down the hallway, past the ugly blue tarp, there was a boy getting high and a girl I was falling pretty hard for. If Joan heard the front door close, she might assume the coast was clear and come out of hiding. I had to get Matt out of my house. "You can go home and call my mother now."

Matt stood there, arms crossed, face muscles taut. "You've put me in a bad situation, Stephen. I'd rather be your youth pastor right now and talk to you about what just happened, but your mom trusted us both this weekend."

"I'm not asking you to not tell on me, okay? You can tell my parents. Heck, I'll tell them myself. I didn't invite Pilar. She found my address online." I opened the front door slowly, sweeping my arm out to make my purpose clear. My shoulder was shrugging every ten seconds or so, but otherwise I was amazingly calm.

"We should talk." Matt wasn't giving in so easily. Probably that was my fault. I let him off the hook for being a glorified babysitter, so he was free to swap "authority figure mode" for "youth minister mode." "Can we sit in the living room?"

"No." I answered too fast, my eyes moving too quickly toward the hallway.

Matt's eyes narrowed, suspicious adult mode activated.

Shit.

"Why not?" He turned from the door, not waiting for an answer.

"Because I don't feel well. I had an upsetting experience emotionally, and I'd like to be alone." I considered faking a spiritual crisis and insisting on talking outside, under the stars, where I was closest to God or some such nonsense, but Matt knew me pretty well. He'd never buy it.

Our house was our house, normal to me, perfect for our three-part family unit, but that night it closed in. As I followed Matt into the living room, the pale wallpaper appeared to move, the lines forming faces that seemed to laugh at me.

I don't know why I ever tried to pull that kind of thing off. I wasn't cut out for lying about parties or getting drunk or sneaking around with girls. All of that was Ballard and who Ballard wanted me to be. After a week of not talking to Ballard, not listening to his insane plans to get laid on prom night or convince Sylvie to give him the time of day, I could clearly see how screwed up our friendship had gotten.

Matt looked around the living room, but it was well and truly empty.

"I told you, I don't feel well." I turned my back on the hypnotic wallpaper.

"Why don't you come home with me? Kelly's almost finished with dinner, and you're supposed to eat with us anyhow." Matt walked toward the kitchen just as I heard it.

Dammit. No.

The tarp moved. It made a distinct swishing sound. I knew what it was, because I heard it all the time. The guys would duck in and out of the construction zone, trailing sawdust and dirt through the hallway. Every evening Mom swept and surveyed the progress.

Matt froze. I froze.

Joan must have heard Pilar leave, but she didn't hear Matt arrive.

My foot kicked out, hitting Matt in the back of his leg, only somewhat on accident.

"Ouch!" He swung around to face me, but immediately turned back at the sound of Nick and Joan practically falling on each other in the hall.

"Come on already, Nick. You shouldn't have come here to start with." Joan's voice was a terse whisper.

"You said that already," Nick told her, louder than he needed to.

Matt and I stood there waiting for the voices' owners to reach us. And they did. Joan drew up short with a gasp. Nick ran into her, and I might've laughed if I hadn't been grimacing something awful and picturing spending the rest of my high school career locked in a closet at The Exchange, allowed only food and prayer books to keep me on the straight and narrow.

Nick looked from me to Matt and grinned. "Hey, dude, the more the merrier."

Joan's light brown skin pinked with embarrassment.

"Hi," she said.

When neither Matt nor I responded, Joan grabbed Nick by the hand and dragged him out the front door. It was all over fast, but not fast enough. My shoulders drooped and I covered my eyes, counting, calming.

"You can explain that over dinner," Matt said.

I had no reason left to argue. I followed him out of my house and down the street to a meal with Kelly in a kitchen that felt more like a holding cell.

Chapter Fifteen

Monday, I went to school exhausted and even more confused than I had been. Over supper at Matt and Kelly's, there'd been lots of talking, but none of it done by me. Mostly Kelly chattered about her friends and her high school days. Matt tried to get me to stay and watch a movie, his way of getting me to relax and talk about things, but I still didn't want to talk.

Except maybe to Joan. I desperately wanted to talk to Joan, to explain how Pilar ended up at my house. I didn't know exactly how I would explain it, because the truth wasn't going to win me any points. But I was done with lying, so when my parents got home Sunday, I told them about Pilar. I mean, I told them I met her at a party at Lake Martin and met up with her at the mall once, but our relationship, or whatever it was, had ended.

I told them Joan came over to keep me company and get away from her sister, which Mom was unsurprised about. When she got over the shock of my having lived a double life the last few weeks, she thanked me for being a friend to Joan. She said it with the same soft look around her eyes that Sylvie sometimes had.

On Monday morning, I headed to school, intent on talking to Joan, and mostly ignoring the fact I was grounded.

Still. And would be grounded indefinitely. Dad yelled. He said some pretty harsh things, but I was used to Dad's tirades. What left me empty was what I heard late Sunday night. The walls of our house were as thin as cotton candy, and I had no trouble hearing everything that happened in the little pantry Dad used as an office. He was in there when I went to bed, typing away, and later I heard Mom go in too.

"You okay?" Dad asked her, his voice kind in a way he rarely offered me.

Mom burst into tears. I'd seen my mother sniffle-cry over sad movies and wipe away stray tears at funerals and weddings, but this was different.

The last time I'd heard my mother cry that way was back in middle school, when my rage came fast and furious, and she was usually the target. My whole body would quake and feel out of my control, and I know now she wanted to help me by offering coping strategies, but then it just felt like she had no idea what she was talking about, like she just wanted to control me, when I couldn't even control me.

And dammit, I cried too, in middle school and Sunday night, covering my mouth to hush the sound. Sometimes I behave like a royal jackass, I know, and it's true Dad makes my blood boil at least 50 percent of the time we're together, but I never meant to hurt my mother. This time, I hadn't thrown anything. No glass shattered in our house. But my lies broke her open just the same.

Ballard met me at the edge of campus. "Still not talking to me?"

I'd double locked Gwinn and was walking with my

head down, noticing a scatter of yellow leaves beneath my shoes. September was past, autumn skirting the edges of our Alabama summer. I didn't answer him, which was answer enough. He sighed but didn't walk away.

"Seriously, man, I was drunk. I didn't mean to throw you under the bus like that."

I don't get why people think being drunk excuses their awful behavior.

We reached the double doors leading into the science wing. I opened one and walked inside, ducking into Chemistry before Ballard had a chance to make more excuses. I didn't get to blame the bad decisions I'd made over the last few weeks on my Tourette's syndrome and I'd be damned if I'd let him blame everything on alcohol.

My next period was Algebra II, and I walked into class ready to talk to Joan, but Joan wasn't there. Sylvie sat by herself at the front of the classroom, tight red jeans tucked into knee-high black boots. The temperature had dipped to seventy, and the slightest gust of wind meant fall in Alabama, time to pull out boots and scarves.

"Where's Joan?" I asked, pausing by Sylvie's desk.

"With Wade." She made a face, scrunching her pouty lips.

I sighed. "What does she see in him?"

Sylvie motioned for me to sit in Joan's empty chair. "You should get her to talk about it, because someone besides me needs to talk sense to her."

"Why would she listen to me?" I opened my notebook as the bell rang and Mr. Collins walked into the classroom.

"She likes you. A lot."

I blushed. “She likes Wade.”

Sylvie shook her head. “No, she’s just sort of attached to Wade. He’s got this hold on her, and he’s a real ass about it. If I were a guy, I’d beat the shit out of him and make him stay away from her. But that’s obviously not happening.” She flexed her nonexistent bicep and laughed sourly.

Sadly, my own biceps weren’t much bigger than Sylvie’s. I rode my bike a lot, sure, but that was more about my legs than my arms. Maybe if someone else held Wade, I could kick him all over and walk away the victor, but there wasn’t much hope of that happening. Besides, Joan didn’t seem like a girl who needed a boy to protect her.

After school, Ballard followed me home, driving at a snail’s pace so he could holler out the window.

“C’mon, man. I said I’m sorry.” He honked, making me jump on the bike seat. “I get it. Even drunk, I shouldn’t have said anything about the experiment. And I wasn’t even that drunk, so I should’ve known better. I’m sorry, Stephen.”

I flipped him the bird.

He sped away and I assumed he’d given up. That hypothesis was incorrect. He was parked at my house, and he knew where Mom kept the extra key, so when I got inside, he was sitting on my bed.

“Listen, I know you’re still pissed, but I did you a favor. Right? I mean, how many girls have you made out with since Sylvie at my party?”

I dropped my backpack on my desk and left the room. Ballard followed.

"And now girls are looking at you differently. Haven't you noticed?"

I could've told him to leave, but Ballard was Ballard. He always got what he wanted, and I was too tired to fight after he admitted the alcohol was no excuse for being such a douche. I opened the fridge and grabbed a Coke. My shoulder jerked, but only once.

The one-jerk tic wasn't so bad. If I paid attention to when it was coming, I could disguise it as a shrug or stretch my arms over my head and yawn so it wasn't as noticeable. At home though, I didn't bother trying to hide my tics. I shouldn't have to care about that stuff inside my own house.

Behind us, there were construction sounds, drills and saws. Somewhere down the hall, Nick Dane was swinging a hammer. My stomach knotted itself and I slumped at the kitchen table.

"Did you hear me?" Ballard had kept talking, but I was focused on Nick being in my house, how he got to rescue Joan when I screwed things up Saturday. "I heard a couple of cheerleaders talking about you today. They said you're cute."

"I don't care, Ballard. I just don't care."

"What do you mean you don't care? Hot girls, bro, talking about you. You, Stephen. And I did that for you."

I laughed, a gravelly sound that echoed into my Coke can as I put it to my lips. I said, "No, Ballard, you didn't do that for me. *I* did that for me."

He crossed the kitchen to get himself a Coke, as at home in my house as I ever was. "Where's your dad? He's usually clicking away in his writing cave."

"I dunno. He's pretty mad at me anyhow. I'm glad he's not here."

Ballard sat down at the table. "What's he mad about?"

I filled him in on everything that came after the party in Beckley Field, my grounding, Pilar showing up . . . I didn't tell him much about Joan though. I didn't tell him I was pretty sure I was in love with her, or how it didn't matter now, since Pilar made sure Joan knew I'd called her a bitch.

Nick appeared in the doorway, re-tying his ponytail, a greasy strand of blond escaping to frame his jaw. He had a thin face, and pale stubble dotted his chin. "Hey, bros, I'm taking a smoke break. Didn't mean to get in the middle of something."

"Nick!" Ballard exclaimed. "Hey, man. I saw the truck outside and was going to ask Stephen if you were here. How's Melody?"

"Who?" Nick tilted his head, fingers already playing with a pack of cigarettes.

"Melody, the girl you were with at that party Saturday night. She was smokin'." Ballard stood and we followed Nick outside.

"Last night . . ." Nick lit his cigarette and took a slow pull. "Melody . . ."

"Oh, come on, bro, the girl you left with was stacked." Ballard accepted a cigarette from Nick.

I waved the pack away, breathing heavy.

"Oh, her." Nick handed Ballard his lighter.

"Since when do you smoke?" I asked, my mouth twisting.

Ballard shrugged and lit the cigarette. One drag and he was coughing up his lungs.

Nick laughed. "Slow down, dude."

Ballard caught his breath and looked sheepishly at me. I shook my head. Idiot.

"Was her name Melody? I never asked." Nick leaned back on my front steps, resting on one elbow. "She was fun though, yeah. We had fun."

Ballard stared at Nick like Nick was God. "So you did it?"

Nick laughed again, and Ballard blushed. I'd never seen him look so much like a little kid.

"If that's what you wanna call it, I guess." Nick licked his lips absently.

"So, that's what you do?" My shoulder jerked hard. "You go around with girl after girl, doing whatever you want, not even remembering their names?"

Nick turned his head toward me, calm as anything. "Well, yeah, I guess so. I mean, I haven't heard any of the girls complaining."

"What about Joan?" I asked.

"Joan?" Nick looked confused. "What about Joan?"

"You left here with Joan Saturday night," I reminded him, my blood hot and my brain screaming I needed to get out of this situation before I lost my cool. "You left with Joan."

"Oh, yeah, I did. She gave me a ride home. Joan's good when I need her." His face was swimming in front of me.

My shoulder jerked, but no one noticed because I was already standing, fist flying at Nick Dane's jaw.

Despite my tiny biceps, I hit at a good angle and took Nick by surprise.

"Oh shit." Ballard grabbed my arms and tugged me off the steps. "What the hell, Luckie?"

Nick rubbed his face but made no move to return fire.

"Don't you ever say shit about Joan." The words seethed between my teeth, and I breathed hard.

Nick chuckled. "Not a bad swing, man."

Ballard let go of my arms and we both stared at Nick.

"What?" he said. "I usually deserve it."

The front door opened and Mr. Dane stepped out. "That's enough of a break. Get your lazy ass back to work."

Nick tossed his cigarette to the sidewalk and rubbed it out with his shoe.

Mr. Dane glared. "And pick that up. Reverend Luckie's yard is not your ashtray."

"Yes, sir." Nick gave a mock salute and grabbed the cigarette butt, following his father back into the house.

"What the hell was that about?" Ballard asked.

"Just go home," I told him, my anger already draining. Jealousy had made me punch someone, and I had never punched anyone. "I'm done talking for today."

Ballard stood there for a minute, but when it became clear I wasn't going to say anything, he dug his keys from the pocket of his jeans and walked toward the Jeep in our driveway.

"Okay, fine." He swung the door open. "But tomorrow, at lunch, you are filling me in on whatever that shit was. Got it?"

"Maybe," I said. "Maybe not. You don't rule me, Ballard."

With an exasperated tossing of his hands in the air before

grabbing the wheel, Ballard backed out of my driveway and headed down the road. In the wrong direction.

I waited until he'd had time to turn around, and watched him drive back past my house with a wave. I went inside to grab my phone and out to the garage where Gwinn the Schwinn waited, her green paint familiar and calming. Lost Bridge Trail beckoned. Maybe I could find a clear head again if I pedaled hard enough and far enough.

I'd forgotten I was grounded.

"Shit," I muttered, standing there just staring at my bike.

That's when the garage door started its grinding ascent. Dad pulled in and cut the engine.

As he climbed out of the car, I said, "I wasn't leaving. I know I'm grounded."

Dad chuckled. "I know you're not leaving. Recent events excluded, you tend to be a pretty trustworthy kid."

I followed him into the house and opened the fridge to grab a drink.

"I know sixteen is tough," Dad said, dropping his wallet and keys on the counter. "I remember. That's the year I got so mad at my own father I moved out for a month."

"Seriously?" I couldn't imagine Dad running away from home. It sounded overly dramatic.

He shrugged. "Your grandpa wasn't a fan of my girlfriend. In that case, he was right. But I wish he'd let me figure it out on my own. Making her off-limits just made me want her more."

I nodded. I could understand that.

"Anyway, I get it. You're going to make some dumb

decisions at this age. We're going to make sure there are consequences. You will hate it. We hate it too."

I wasn't sure he hated my being grounded as much as I hated me being grounded, but I appreciated the sentiment. Dad and I hadn't talked like this, without his tone tinged in disappointment, in a long time.

"Do me a favor and ride to the corner store, real quick. I need some olive oil to make dinner tonight."

I smiled. "Sure."

As I guided Gwinn out of the garage, I felt a bit better about life.

Chapter Sixteen

As I rode through downtown, my eyes glanced off shop windows. I almost didn't notice the bike, but the lady who runs the thrift store waved from the window. I waved back and caught the sun glinting off handlebars. Immediately, I pulled to the curb, locked up Gwinn, and went inside.

"It was donated this morning," Judy said when I asked about the battered Huffy. It could use a fresh coat of paint, new tires, and some general TLC, but it wasn't in bad shape all in all. I could let Joan know it was there.

Or I could buy it for her.

I pulled out my wallet. Dad paid me for yard work, and Mom paid me for cleaning the church office sometimes. I mostly spent my money on music and I'd saved for my guitar. I had enough for the bike.

"It's a girl's bike," Judy pointed out.

I blushed and my fingers flexed around the cash. "I know. It's not for me."

Judy grinned. "Girlfriend?"

My cheeks were Alabama crimson. "Just a friend. Can I pay you now and pick it up later?"

Judy took my money and moved the bike to the back storeroom. I thanked her and hopped back on Gwinn the Schwinn, heading for the Tallapoosa.

Like I'd summoned her with my brain, there was Joan's car, parked near the bridge. Knowing she wouldn't be on the bridge, due to her confessed fear, I turned onto a thin trail leading down the hill. I had to get off the bike and walk to keep from sliding and breaking Gwinn and me both.

The sound of gravel and footsteps alerted her to my presence, and Joan turned around. She was standing near the riverbank, Sylvie beside her. Sylvie waved, and I stopped to wave back. For a minute, I watched them, unsure of what to say once I got close. Joan's arms were crossed, her electric-blue T-shirt bunched around the waist. She'd freshened up the streak in her hair, so it matched the shirt perfectly. She looked amazing.

"How'd you do on the *Gatsby* test?" Sylvie asked when I finally approached them.

"I got an A, thanks to Joan." I offered Joan a smile she didn't return.

"Did you really call me a bitch to that girl?" Her face was stone, and I tried not to picture how she smiled, giggled, leaving my house with Nick.

"Yes." I know, I could've denied it. Pilar's word against mine.

Joan knew too. "You could at least lie."

"Stephen is one of the last honest people we know," Sylvie said, paraphrasing Fitzgerald.

I took a deep breath. My fingers flexed on the handlebars, and I squeezed the rubber grips, the grooves mashing into my skin. Joan could be so scary, but right then, I wasn't afraid of her.

"I could lie, yeah, but I won't. I'm done lying. The first truth is, I called you a bitch so Pilar wouldn't guess the second truth, which is that I have always been a little bit in love with you. You have always been strong and confident in a no-holds-barred, take-no-prisoners, I'm-gonna-be-myself-and-if-you-don't-like-me-fuck-you kind of way."

My not-so-Shakespearean monologue hung between us. Sylvie smirked, and I knew I'd made the right choice, being honest. But Joan didn't smirk or smile or even frown. She just stared.

Sylvie nudged Joan. Joan stepped away from her friend, closer to me. "Were you that honest with Pilar Saturday night?"

I nodded. "I'm not sure she appreciated it. Or believed me. But, yes. I took your advice and told her the truth."

Joan uncrossed her arms. "I don't like name calling. Don't do it again."

"I won't."

"All right, then. Sylvie and I are going for milkshakes at the Dairy Cream. Want to come?"

"I'm still grounded," I said. "Dad turns a blind eye to the occasional bike ride, but I don't think I can get away with the Dairy Cream."

Joan helped me get my bike back up the steep incline. She and Sylvie were almost to her car and I was a few yards away when I turned around to yell back at them.

"Hey, Joan!"

"Yeah?" She shielded her eyes from the afternoon sun with one hand, her other dangling car keys.

"When's your birthday?" I was thinking about the bike, about painting it the same shade of pink as her car.

"Why?"

"Because I wanna know." I laughed at the confused look on her face. I hoped she'd say January or April or something, a date far away.

"October thirteenth."

"Thanks!" As I turned to ride away, I couldn't help but feel lucky.

Yeah, yeah, I said it. Lucky.

I was pretty lucky that day. No one was home when I pulled into the driveway. I locked Gwinn in the garage and made a snack before math homework. The rest of my grounding pitter-pattered away, filled with days at school and afternoons helping Mom at The Exchange. I avoided Nick Dane like the plague, but that failed a time or two, what with him practically living in my house, running power tools and looking entirely too pleased with himself on a regular basis.

A week or so into October, my parents announced my grounding was over.

I hurried home after school and was glad to see Mom's car in the driveway.

"Can you take me to Auburn? I need to go to the bike shop." I hadn't even dropped my backpack onto the kitchen table. I went straight to where Mom sat on her bed with a giant Bible commentary and her sermon-writing notebook.

"Not today. I ended up in meetings all morning. I'm

behind now." She didn't even look up from the page she was studying.

"Is Dad going to be home soon? It's really important." I bounced slightly from foot to foot.

"He's in Montgomery for an appointment." She raised her head from the book and examined my face, which had to be glowing, I was so ready to burst. "What's got you so anxious?"

"I need to get paint and some parts for a project. It's time sensitive."

"I suppose you can take my car."

She hadn't let me drive to Auburn before, always claiming it was too far, but maybe my need to get out of the house that day fit with her need for a quiet space to work. Whatever the reason, she handed me her keys. I attached the new used bicycle to the rack and hit the road. I called on the way, so Allen had what I needed ready and waiting when I arrived.

"Pink?" The cashier raised an eyebrow. It was thc same cashier who offered to call 911 back in August.

"It's not for me," I told her, and she smiled.

I smiled back. Grinned actually. Joan and I had been talking almost daily since I confessed both loving and hating her. There wasn't anything romantic. But I had hope.

I loaded my purchases into the trunk, and my phone buzzed with a text from Joan.

You're free now, right?

I am!

Good. Can you help me study for the chem midterm?

I'm in Auburn. Let me get back to town and I can. Library?

Can you come to the house? Pearl borrowed my car.

No problem. See you in an hour or so.

I headed back home to stash the bike and all of my repair supplies. While there, I washed my face, put on extra deodorant, and brushed my teeth.

I was pretty sure Joan's parents weren't home, and if Pearl was gone with the car, that meant Joan and I were going to be alone in her room. I would help her study for the Chemistry test. But, at the risk of being a cheesy cliché, I hoped to make a little chemistry of our own.

No spin-the-bottle app on my phone, and no mad scientist make-out experiment necessary.

I was finally going to kiss Joan Pearson.

Joan lived in a brick house on the outskirts of town, a mile from the interstate. When I pulled in, I noticed the Great Dane Construction truck across the street. Nick was standing beside it, smoking, and Joan was sitting in the passenger seat with the door open. Music spilled from radio speakers, and Joan hopped out to walk toward me.

"Later, Nick," she called over her shoulder. Then she smiled at me.

My heart hit my throat and my fingers flexed, so I stuck my hands in my pockets. For the last week, my tics were so calm even my father commented. Mom said maybe I didn't need a neuro appointment after all. It felt nice, good, but not for the reasons I though it would.

When we started the kissing experiment, I wanted my tics to stop so a girl might like me. Now that I knew the tics didn't keep girls from liking me, I enjoyed the calm because it was a side effect of not being stressed as shit. I was happy because I was happy, not because I was using make-out sessions to control my body.

I followed Joan inside and down a hall. She opened her bedroom door and turned back to motion me inside. Looking around her bedroom, I was startled. I don't know what I expected, but that wasn't it.

"I know, I know. I haven't changed it since I was, like, ten. But I like it. It's cozy." Joan sat on the foot of her bed while I spun in a slow circle, a half smile tickling my lips.

The walls were papered with pink and yellow flowers, and a floor to ceiling shelf held row after row of dolls.

"I used to collect American Girl stuff," Joan told me. "Furniture, clothes, books, you name it. The attic's overflowing."

"American Girl," I repeated.

Joan patted the bed beside her, and I sat. I tore my eyes from the dolls and noticed a series of drawings framed on another wall.

"You like them?" Joan walked over and removed one from its nail. She handed it to me.

In strokes of ink, someone had drawn Cinderella, complete with blue dress and glass slippers. Only, in this version, Cinderella was Korean.

"Wade did them."

Joan couldn't have shocked me more if she'd revealed they were drawn by the orange cat sleeping on her pillow.

"Wade Bond drew this?"

She nodded. "He does them for my birthday and Christmas

every year, because I complained once about the lack of Asian girls in Disney movies."

Behind her head, there was Sleeping Beauty, Snow White, Jasmine, and Alice from *Alice in Wonderland*.

"I have more that aren't framed yet." She took Cinderella from my hands and hung it back on the wall.

"I didn't know Wade could draw."

She shrugged. "He doesn't show anyone. His dad says it's a waste of time and he should stick to football."

"It's not a waste of time," I said.

"Of course not." She sat beside me. "But Wade's parents have certain expectations. He's not always what he looks like to you."

"In middle school. You punched Wade in the face, and I never thanked you. I'm sorry I got so pissed about it."

She sighed. "You said I made it worse."

"Yeah, you did, but you didn't mean to. It's not your fault Wade's an asshole." I picked up her hand and studied it, the smooth skin and her gold Celtic knot ring. I turned her hand in mine and ran a finger over the longest line on her palm.

"Can we not talk about Wade right now?" Her words were a whisper.

Goose bumps appeared on her skin as my finger trailed across her wrist.

Joan shifted onto her knees and leaned in close. Her hair swung around my face, the tips tickling my neck. I set my hands on her waist, my fingers pressing into skin where her shirt didn't quite meet her jeans.

I wasn't tic-ing at all.

For a minute, we held that pose, and if you could kiss someone with your eyes, that would be what we were doing. Then the staring went from romantic to awkward as I cleared my throat and the sound reverberated.

I broke the stare, blushing, and let my gaze land on her lips, pink and shiny, and then I tugged her forward and her mouth was so soft, and the perfect weight of her settled in my lap like a dream.

Joan's teeth tugged at my bottom lip, her cold and perfect fingers slid through my hair, and our tongues tasted each other slowly.

When we pulled apart, it was no longer just me blushing, and I didn't even mind all of those dolls watching us watch each other.

I leaned forward so we were forehead to forehead, and asked, "Can we do that again?"

"And again and again," Joan said.

And so we did.

Chapter Seventeen

The days after Joan and I finally kissed passed like a dream. I practically floated to my classes, seeing Joan in the halls, holding her hand, kissing her when I was brave enough.

We hung out at her house in the evenings, so she could be home if her dad called. He didn't call. He'd checked himself into rehab and wouldn't be allowed to use the phone for a while. Her mom was nice to me and even invited me to dinner some nights.

There were other things that weren't great in those days though. Mainly, my conscience, so I went looking for Erin.

I found her leaving a classroom on the second floor, walking with Joan. We hadn't spoken since I got grounded over the whole drunk party thing, so I wasn't surprised when she ducked her head and turned away.

"Wait, can we talk? For just a minute?" I followed her past a few lockers.

She paused, glanced toward Joan, and then nodded. "Yeah, we should talk, I guess. I'm sorry about ratting on you. I wasn't trying to get you in trouble. I didn't know Kelly would call your mom."

Joan stepped closer to me and took my hand. She smiled at Erin, tipping her head in acknowledgment.

"I get it, mostly, but why didn't you just talk to me?"

Erin shrugged, which didn't help at all.

"Did I do something, before this, to make you think you couldn't tell me what was bothering you?"

"Not really, Stephen. Some things aren't about you. I had to talk to someone, about more than just that party with you. Kelly was there."

I nodded.

"And I did try to talk to you, but it turned into a fight. I'd had enough fighting with boys."

"Okay," I said. "You're right. I wasn't helpful."

"Erin!" Someone called her name from down the hall.

Erin shot a relieved look over her shoulder. "That's my lab partner. I need to get to Chemistry." She turned to Joan. "Thanks, for what you said."

Joan shrugged. "It's only true."

"Yeah, but thanks for saying it."

And then Erin disappeared into the crowd of students, and I put my arm around Joan's waist as we walked the other way. "What did you say to her?"

"Nothing much," Joan said. "Just that she's too smart to let a guy control her emotions. You know, the kind of thing Sylvie said to me for months before I finally let Wade go."

We were standing outside of her History class when one of Wade's friends walked by. He paused at the sight of us and turned to holler over the crowd.

"Hey, Luckie, be careful. I hear she still lets Wade visit the penguins."

Before I could figure out what he was talking about, he laughed and ducked into a classroom.

I turned to Joan, and she was quivering. Her whole body shook.

"What is it?" I asked. "What was he talking about?"

"Wade's such a bastard," she said, but she was sobbing so hard it sounded more like, "Wabe is"—*gasp*—"sush a"—*gasp*—"bastard." The last word was clear, and that was all I needed. I took her hand and dragged her down the hall and out the door.

It was the first time I ever cut school. I took Joan's keys and drove her home. She texted her mom that she wasn't feeling well, and I sat with her on her bed while she cried.

"He lied," she said when the tears reached an end. "He said he never told anyone, but he lied."

"Wade?" I asked.

She nodded.

I brushed a stray tear from her eyelashes. She tucked her head underneath my chin.

"The first time Wade and I had sex, I was wearing a bra with stupid little cartoon penguins on it. I was embarrassed, and he teased me. I mean, if I'd planned to have sex that night, I would've worn a different bra, right? After, whenever he wanted to have sex, he'd ask if he could visit the penguins."

"If I were about to have sex with you," I said, "I wouldn't care if there were penguins or ostriches or flying pink flamingos on your bra."

She laughed. "There are no birds on any of my bras anymore."

I made a playful tug on her shirt hem. "Can I check?"

"Not yet," she said. But she looked at me and smiled, and making her smile was the best thing I'd ever done. It was even better than kissing her.

Okay, never mind, nothing was better than kissing her.

So I kissed her. I kissed her for a long time, and by the time she drove me back to the school to pick up my bike, I knew she'd told the truth. There were no birds on her bra, only little white polka dots on the red cotton.

The next day, I was nervous. Sylvie brought Joan's birthday gift to school. She got her a necklace with an ice cream cone pendant. Joan said it was an inside joke, or not a joke exactly, but there was a story and she'd tell me sometime. She put it on immediately.

I'd shown up empty-handed. It's not like I could bring the bike with me. How would I ride two bikes to school, and what would Joan do with it all day? It sure wasn't going to fit in a locker or her little pink Beetle. It would have to be a later gift. I enlisted Ballard's help to get it where I wanted it when I needed it to be there. We'd only talked a little since he showed up at my house and I punched Nick, but I was feeling too happy to hold my grudge.

We were standing near the library, Sylvie and Ballard talking about Ballard's party coming up over the weekend. She was helping him plan it, and she promised to "class it up" a notch.

Joan and I were holding hands, listening to our friends argue about the need for cocktail napkins and floating lanterns. I loved how Sylvie brought out an almost romantic side of Ballard, and Joan said it was great to see Sylvie acting more like a teenager. They fit together. It was weird.

Someone tapped Joan on the shoulder and she turned around.

Wade.

"Happy birthday," he told her, holding out a bouquet of semi-wilted pink carnations.

Joan stared at the flowers, her lips set in a hard straight line. She looked to be debating her next move. It would either be spit in his face or knee him in the balls.

I took the flowers from his hands.

He glared at me.

"Hey, moron, those aren't for you."

I took a step past Joan and dropped the ugly flowers into a big navy-blue trash can. No one said a word as I rejoined the group. Joan covered her mouth, suppressing a giggle. Wade's face swirled like a lava lamp as various shades of blue and red and purple took turns shadowing his features.

A teacher opened the library door, almost knocking Wade in the face. He tripped backward, righted himself, and came toward me.

"Mr. Bond, you were supposed to be here ten minutes ago. You will never pass if you don't show up to tutoring."

The teacher crossed his arms, and Joan lost her battle, letting the laughter escape. Wade's head snapped toward her.

"You're an asshole, Wade," Joan said, but her anger was mixed with happiness now. I'd made her smile again.

"Joan, are you . . ." He paused and looked me over before finishing. "Are you seriously dating this dork?"

Joan took my hand and squeezed it. "I am."

"What a waste."

"Mr. Bond, the only thing currently being wasted is my time. Let's go." The teacher walked back into the library and Wade turned to follow, head down.

"Hey, Wade," Joan called.

He looked over his shoulder. "What?"

"I'm going to let Stephen visit the penguins. I bet they'll like him better."

Probably, antagonizing Thor isn't a good idea. My guess is that thunder gods hold grudges. But we could deal with that later.

After school, Ballard met me at the house, cover off his Jeep, and we loaded Gwinn the Schwinn and the refurbished pink bicycle. Ballard pulled away and I went inside. Nick Dane was leaning against my bedroom door.

"Hey, bro," he said.

"Hi, Nick." I crossed my arms.

"Look, man, I'm sorry I gave you the wrong idea. You know, about Joan and me. I didn't know, you know?"

"Didn't know what?" I raised an eyebrow.

"That you, you know, were into her."

How many times could this guy say "you know" in a five-second span?

"Joan's cool. And she likes you, man. Be good to her, okay?" Nick eyed me like a possible danger, like he was Joan's stand-in father, sizing me up and cleaning his shotgun.

"Of course." My fingers flexed in my pocket. My tics had been pretty calm over the last week or so, like sheer happiness was all it took to relax my nerves. I know that isn't the case. When I'm stressed, it's true, my tics get worse, but not being stressed doesn't mean they go entirely away.

"Can I get into my room now, please?"

"Yeah, man, sure. We're almost done back here. Dad's painting now."

They weren't done enough for me to use the new bathroom though. I grabbed my shower stuff and slipped into the old one, shaving despite little need for it, and putting on a dark green shirt. It was long-sleeved. The temp was dropping a touch, which is about the extent of fall in Alabama.

When Joan rang the doorbell, Mom was home. She'd come in through the garage door and shot me a questioning look.

"I know it's a school night," I answered her unasked question. "But it's Joan's birthday. I'm giving her the bike down by the trail."

She'd watched me work on the bike in our garage. Once she spotted the pink paint, I had no choice but to explain. She nodded. "Have fun, and don't be out too late."

When I opened the door, Joan kissed my cheek and waved at my mother. "Hey, Reverend Luckie."

"Please, call me Renee." Mom smiled at Joan.

Joan and I got into her car.

"So, what's the surprise?" Joan asked.

"You'll see," I told her. "Drive to Lost Bridge Park."

Joan was good at surprises. She didn't ask any more questions.

When we reached the bridge across the Tallapoosa, I

watched her whole body change. Her knuckles went white on the steering wheel. Her breathing sped up and she stared hard, straight ahead. I reached across the console and put a hand lightly on her knee. Her muscles relaxed, but barely.

When we exited the bridge, she took a deep breath. "That is so embarrassing."

"Why do bridges scare you so bad?"

She shrugged. "I don't know. I never had any traumatic experience on one. But I have nightmares about them collapsing."

"That would be terrifying," I admitted.

"It is," she said. "And I don't know if the nightmares are because I'm scared of bridges, or if bridges scare me because of the nightmares."

It wasn't far from the Tallapoosa to Lost Bridge Park. We passed Ballard leaving the lot, but Joan didn't notice the Jeep. We parked, and I held her hand as we walked toward the trailhead, where the bikes were locked to a tree.

Gwinn looked the same as always, green paint a little in need of cleaning. The pink bike glistened brand new, and there was a yellow ribbon tied in a bow on the handlebars. Mom tied the bow after my fifth attempt failed.

"Happy birthday," I said, suddenly nervous she would hate it.

She looked from the bike to my face. "That's for me?"

I nodded. "Yeah, I found it in the thrift store, and I fixed it up, painted it to match your car—"

"Oh, Stephen!" She grinned wide, cheeks pink and dark

eyes sparking like flint. She threw her arms around me, and I laughed.

Once I'd unlocked both bikes and stashed the chains in her car, we pedaled off into the woods. As we rode, we talked about Ballard's party and whether or not we should do one of those cheesy couple costumes. I was relieved she didn't want to, because I didn't either, but if she'd said she wanted to, I would've done it. I wouldn't tell Joan no. I wanted to say yes to her, over and over and over, give her anything she wanted.

Yes. Yes. Yes. Yes. Yes.

A mile into the ride, we topped a small hill and there it was, Lost Bridge.

Joan braked, and I stopped beside her.

"We can turn back," I offered.

She shook her head. "I don't let fear win. Ever."

"Okay, then, if you're serious, we can't ride over it fast either."

"What do you mean?" Her head tilted, eyes locked on the wooden slats. It had rained the day before, so the creek was full and rushing.

I leaned my bike against a tree and motioned for her to do the same. She did, and when I took her hand it was trembling.

"Over water is the worst." She tightened her grip the closer we got. "Bridges on the interstate aren't so bad, but when there's water . . ."

"Shh . . . ," I said. "Don't think. Just walk."

"That's easy for you to say. You aren't scared of anything."

I stopped and looked at her. "Are you kidding?"

She shook her head.

"I'm scared of everything. All the time. Hell, Joan, until recently, I was scared of you."

She tore her eyes from the bridge two feet away and met my eyes. "Me?"

I walked forward, holding her attention the best I could. "Yes, you. You are gorgeous and strong and wild and free, and I am, well, me. You can be pretty intimidating."

She smiled again, and I stopped walking. "Look."

She glanced around and froze. "Shit."

I took her other hand and pulled her facing me. We were dead center of Lost Bridge. If we looked down, we would see Lost Creek stampeding beneath our feet. We didn't look down though. We looked at each other.

"Are you scared?" I asked.

She nodded.

"I'm right here," I whispered in her ear, my arms locked around her waist. "I won't let go."

She tugged at my shirt, her fingers tangled in the fabric, and I held on tighter.

"Stephen," she said into my chest.

"Yeah?"

"What if my dad doesn't get better?"

I ran my fingers along her spine, pressing into each knot of bone, the pieces that held her together, made her stand tall. I was holding Joan's pride in my hands, and I had to be careful not to break it.

"I believe he will," I told her. "But if he doesn't, you'll be okay. Better than okay, because you're strong."

“I don’t feel strong.” She pulled her head back, our bodies tight together and eyes locked.

“You are.” I pressed my palm against her spine. “Feel that?”

“Yes.” Her voice was so low, so quiet, I barely heard it.

“That’s you, Joan. When you fall down, you always get back up, and nothing your dad does can change that. Nothing Wade says about you can be true so long as you stand up straight. He doesn’t get to win.”

“He doesn’t?”

I smiled. “Nope. He doesn’t. We win, Joan. *We* win.”

And I kissed her there, in the middle of her worst fears, her body going soft and easy in my arms. The sound of the creek disappeared. Wade and her father disappeared. Pilar and Erin and Ballard and Nick. Everyone was gone but me and her.

As we walked to our bikes, Joan put her hand on my back and I paused. She ran her fingers slowly up my spine, tingles shooting over every inch of me. “Feel that?”

“Yes,” I answered.

“You’re strong too, Stephen. You’re strong enough to keep me from breaking, and I didn’t think anyone was strong enough for that.”

We got back on the bikes, and when we rode across Lost Bridge, Joan Pearson was grinning at me.

Chapter Eighteen

The Halloween party fell on a cool night, rain threatening but not quite leaving the clouds. Joan wore black jeans, a black sweater, and a headband with cat ears. I picked her up in Mom's car and drove us to Lake Martin while she scrolled through radio stations. Our being together had become comfortable without ever losing the spark that made me grin anytime she looked my way.

As we walked toward the front door, I spotted Wade by the water's edge and shuddered with a sense of déjà vu. He didn't trip me though, didn't even notice Joan and me darting past.

Once inside, I grabbed us a couple of sodas, neither Joan nor me wanting to repeat the drunken shenanigans we'd indulged in at our last party. As usual, the front room was full of people playing *Call of Duty* on the giant screen TV. Joan found Sylvie, and the two of them flitted off to the bathroom.

Left on my own, I wandered into the dining room and was surprised to find Pilar and her cousin from Moorhen, Luz, watching some guys set up beer pong. Luz glared when she spotted me, but Pilar only looked wary.

My fingers flexed against my Coke can. I didn't know what to say but needed to say something. My ability to talk to girls should've improved after the last month, but it hadn't. I mumbled something incoherent, and Pilar raised her eyebrows.

"Sorry," I said, more clearly. "Could I maybe talk to you a minute?"

"I'm listening." She didn't move toward the door. She wasn't going to make this easy.

The beer pong boys went on arranging tiny red cups, and Luz watched me squirm.

"So, um, we didn't part on the best of terms." I tried to suppress a jerk of my left shoulder.

Pilar harrumphed and Luz rolled her eyes.

"I just wanted to say I'm sorry. I was a clueless douche, and I should've respected you enough to be honest from the very beginning."

"Yeah, you should have," Pilar said.

As though on cue, Joan appeared beside me in the doorway. She grabbed my hand and wove our fingers together, squeezing.

Pilar's eyes trailed down my arm, paused at Joan's hand gripping mine, and then traveled back to my face. "Yeah, well, it's over now. Whatever. I'm not sitting around pining for you or anything."

"I hope you can forgive me," I told her.

Pilar shrugged. "You were right that we weren't officially together to begin with. But we weren't not together either, Stephen. Relationships aren't black and white, and I can't just snap my fingers and forgive you."

"I know," I said, fingers flexing against Joan's hand. I did know. People were always thinking I should be able to decide to change and then change, just like that, and I was never able to please them. The brain and the heart were not electronics with on-and-off switches. "I know, Pilar. I just . . ."

"I get it," she said. "You're sorry. You never meant to hurt me and all that."

"I *didn't* mean to hurt you."

"And I didn't mean to let you. But it happened. Maybe I will forgive you. Maybe I won't. That's my decision, and you will just have to live with it, either way."

Joan gave my hand an encouraging squeeze.

"I'm sorry, Pilar," I said again.

"Yeah, me too. Let's just move on now." Pilar's eyes were already leaving my face and following one of the beer pong guys. He smiled at her, and she blushed.

"Yeah, all right," I said, and Joan tugged me out of the doorway, leading me around the corner to the den, where we set our sodas on the coffee table and settled on the loveseat. She leaned her head on my shoulder.

"You feel any better?" Joan asked.

"A bit." My brain replayed all of the mistakes I'd made with Pilar. "I wish I could undo some things."

Joan turned her head to look up at me. "We all make mistakes."

"Maybe. Mine were pretty bad though."

"Yeah, you acted pretty dumb. I mean, look how long it took for you to get around to kissing me." She grinned.

"I promise, I've learned my lesson." I kissed Joan's grinning lips and she wrapped her arms around my neck. I'd never known you could have that much fun at a party, or I would've shown up at every one I got invited to.

It was nearing midnight when Joan and I walked onto the deck. We'd mostly been talking by ourselves all evening, but now we decided to join the crowd outside.

Sylvie had strung orange twinkle lights around the rails of the deck, and I could see a row of lanterns bobbing on the water. She'd told Joan and me she wanted to make this high school party more mature. I spotted her sitting on Ballard's lap on an Adirondack chair near the fire pit. King and queen of the party scene, just like they were always meant to be. It seemed strange that I ever questioned them as a couple, now that they were so obviously a matched set. Sylvie looked relaxed and happy, and Ballard wasn't even drunk.

When Joan spotted a friend and broke away, I walked toward Ballard. My toes were flexing inside my shoes, but it was a minor annoyance, nothing I couldn't deal with. The sounds of Post Malone drowned out the conversations around us, and Ballard had to practically yell to ask how my night was going.

"It's great," I yelled back.

I sat with them a while, thinking about how much had changed in the months since the last party at Ballard's. That night, I just wanted to disappear, to blend in, to be normal, but normal isn't so clear anymore. Everyone I saw on that deck was dealing with something, and a lot of them thought and acted differently than one another, once I slowed down and paid attention. Even Wade, with his secret princess sketches for

Joan and his struggles with math. It turns out neurodiversity isn't just about me being different. It's about everyone being allowed to be themselves. Freely and truly. I wasn't sure that was possible for all of the kids in Moorhen, but it was possible for me, because I had good friends and finally accepted myself exactly as I was.

After a while, I went looking for Joan. She was in a far corner of the deck, sitting on a lounge chair by herself.

I sat down and leaned against the back of the lounge chair. Joan leaned her body against mine. She took off her cat-ear headband, rubbing her temples, and tossed it to the side. Her head fit perfectly in the crook of my neck, and she smelled like lake water and mint gum. Above us, a set of silver wind chimes sparkled in the twinkle lights, a breeze eliciting the soft tangle of tunes.

In the distance, over the sound of another Post Malone song, I heard Ballard's loud laugh and a shriek as someone got thrown into the water, but it was the wind chimes that mesmerized Joan and me. We watched them dancing above us, and I kissed the top of Joan's head, right where her dark hair parted to reveal a line of warm brown skin.

"Can we stay like this forever?" Joan asked, her voice dreamy.

"Yes," I said. "We can."

Acknowledgments

First things first, by the time this is on a shelf, Corey will have spent twenty years married to me, and being married to a writer is no easy road. Thank you for loving me, even when I basically have to exist in another world for hours and weeks on end in order to make a book.

Thanks, Mom, for reading all of my manuscripts and telling me how awesome they are. Thanks, Dad, for giving me stories as a child and encouraging my melodramatic teenage poetry. Thanks to my steps, Wayne, Candy, Linda, Tara, and David, for being way more than steps to me. Thank you to my sons, Haydn and David, for listening to my plot issues, indulging my strange teen-culture questions, and always being willing to make me dinner while I work. Thank you to my stepdaughter, Savannah. The story I wrote that made me believe I can do this . . . it was the sci-fi novella I wrote for your eleventh birthday. To my brothers: Jimmy, I love you, and Danny, I miss you. To my baby sister: Carrie, you were my first reader. I still have one story I wrote for you when we were kids. It's ridiculous, but you loved it, and I love you. Thanks for being my cheerleader, always.

I have so many amazing friends who have listened to me vent and brainstorm throughout this process. I can't possibly name them all. Leila, your friendship saved me in ways you'll never know. I wouldn't be healthy enough to write without you. Louise, I always know you are praying for me and rooting for my success. To the Clines, thank you for cabin time to finish revisions and plenty of drinks and laughs. To Jen Hawkins and Mara Rutherford, thank you for your writerly solidarity on those never-gonna-sell-a-book days.

I also have a lot of amazing groups where I am accepted and inspired, writer-centric and otherwise: TOT/ Pitchwars 2014, the Clubhouse, Swoon Squad, the 21ders, the Kick Ass Girls Group, The Well @ Lewisburg, Thick and the Dead, and all of my #ActuallyAutistic groups and friends.

I had a lot of readers along the way. Thank you: Kim Lawson, Dee Garretson, Jennifer Park, Alison Miller, Alexandra Alessandri, Sonia Hartl, Lindsay Portwood, Amanda Hill, and Dannie Morin. Thanks to all of you who read this story while it was on the Swoon website as well. Your comments helped in the revision process. There are also plenty of people and places that helped me with this story or inspired parts of it: Izzie, Trails & Treads (bike rental), Middle Sisters (meet-up at Lake Martin), the generous people who shared their experiences with TS, and the handful of teens who helped me with pop-culture stuff (especially Olivia Holloway).

Finally, this book started with a lot of editorial help from Amy Tipton before it landed on the Swoon website. My agent, Hilary Harwell, has been a godsend as I navigate the editorial process as a debut author. I have been lucky enough to work on this book with Kat Brzozowski, Holly Ingraham, and Lauren Scobell. Swoon is full of fabulous people, and I am so grateful to be part of the squad.

P.S. A special thank-you to Edna St. Vincent Millay, Shere Khan, and Sir Terry Pratchett, the kitties that keep me company as I write.

Check out more books chosen for publication by readers like you.